SHERLOCK HOLMES at the 1902 FIFTH TEST

History records that Wednesday the 13th of August 1902 was one of English cricket's most glorious days, when England recovered from a disastrous position against the Australians in the Oval Test Match and snatched victory from the very jaws of defeat. However, history does not record that, without Sherlock Holmes this sporting triumph would not have been possible.. But for the intervention of the Great Detective there would have been no match-winning last wicket partnership between George Hirst and Wilfred Rhodes—*for Rhodes himself was not at the Oval on the day in question.*

SHERLOCK HOLMES at the
1902 FIFTH TEST

SHERLOCK HOLMES
at the
1902 FIFTH TEST

by
Stanley Shaw

MAGNA PRINT BOOKS
Long Preston, North Yorkshire,
England.

British Library Cataloguing in Publication Data.

Shaw, Stanley, *1922—*
    Sherlock Holmes at the 1902 fifth test.
    I. Title
    823'.914 (F)

    ISBN 1-85057-539-8
    ISBN 1-85057-540-1 pbk

First Published in Great Britain by W.H. Allen & Co. PLC 1985

Published in Large Print 1989 by arrangement with W.H. Allen & Co. Ltd., London.

Printed and bound in Great Britain by
Redwood Burn Limited, Trowbridge, Wiltshire.

The following is an extract from a letter sent by a widowed lady, living in Gloucestershire, to the Secretary of the Holmes/Watson Society.

'The enclosed handwritten memoir, and typescript copy of same, will be of interest to you. The memoir was found amongst a wealth of miscellaneous papers—my late father's—kept in an old trunk. I had sorted through these papers shortly after his death at the age of eighty-six, but I somehow overlooked the packet containing it. Now, some twenty years later, my grand-daughter has unearthed it. I read a portion of it—my eyesight not being what it was—and decided it was so interesting it would be worthwhile asking my grand-daughter to make a type-written copy of it, and this she did. I was then able to read it in its entirety.

'It is a very curious tale indeed. I shall be on tenterhooks until I hear what you make of it....'

CHAPTER ONE

The White Star liner, s.s *Athenic*, sailed from Melbourne, towards the end of June, 1902, and I, John Fairhurst, was one of the two hundred and seventy passengers.

Five weeks later the ship had emerged from the Suez Canal and was in the Mediterranean. Soon we should pass through the Straits of Gibraltar and enter upon the final stage of our voyage to England.

But—hullo!—going to the rail after breakfast one day we passengers saw land visible both to port and to starboard. It could not be Gibraltar so soon. Well, the rumour flew about that we were in the Straits of Messina. A glance at the tattered shilling atlas I had brought with me told me that, if that were so, we were steaming northward into the

Tyrrhenian Sea, bound for the Italian port of Naples. At noon the rumour was admitted to be undoubted fact. We were diverting to Naples to pick up a handful of extra passengers.

I am sure the majority of passengers were delighted to be afforded the opportunity of feasting their eyes on a panoramic view of the Bay of Naples—reputed to be one of the most beautiful views in the world. For myself, I was not at all pleased with this turn of events. If it resulted in the ship arriving at its destination several days after its scheduled date of arrival it would be too late for me to be present at the Kennington Oval cricket ground, in South London, to watch the Fifth (and final) Test Match of the 1902 series between England and Australia.

Eventually we did indeed steam into the Bay of Naples. Despite my feelings of resentment I had to acknowledge the breathtaking beauty of the vista as we approached the Santa Lucia waterfront and cast anchor. A small band of musicians stood on the cause-

10

way that joined the great Castell dell' Ovo fortress to the mainland, and the lilting strains of the familiar melody, 'Santa Lucia', floated across the intervening three or four hundred yards of water.

Apparently the extra passengers came aboard. I never saw them as I chanced to be below at the time. Several hours elapsed, and all the time I was impatient for us to be away and out to sea, but another rumour flew about. It was said that three of the crew had slipped ashore without permission and that, therefore, the same number of officers had been sent to scour the waterfront for them and bring them back.

The light was beginning to fade when, greeted with ironical cheers from passengers leaning over the rail, a small ship's boat appeared, and it was noted that there were six men in it.

One of the apprehended crewmen was plainly very much the worse for drink. As he climbed the ladder to get on board he took one hand off the side-rail to wave a farewell to the hospitable port of Naples and that proved to be his undoing. He fell headlong downwards, seeming to strike his head a glancing blow on the gunwale of the ship's boat below. I heard laughter all around me, but I was concerned for the man and when, after ten or fifteen seconds, he had not come to the surface, I climbed swiftly on to the rail and dived into the water.

The force of my entry into the harbour depths dragged up my light poplin jacket so that when I, with difficulty, struggled to the surface I felt as if I were in a straitjacket. Nevertheless I gulped in air and plunged down.

I saw no sign of anyone, kicked out and came up. The drunken crewman, I then saw, was standing and swaying on the lower rungs of the ship's ladder, his head turned towards me. When I began to flounder in that direction, still hampered by my jacket, he reached out a hand to assist me. Immediately I heard a roar of laughter from above and it struck me that, far from cutting the heroic figure of a rescuer, I was a laughing-stock.

Eventually we arrived on deck, dripping wet, and the crewman was hustled away, doubtless for some kind of retribution. I made my way down below deck and into a bath cubicle as quickly as I could, and as I bathed, soaping away the harbour-slime, I felt sore about the outcome of my impetuous leap from the rail. On deck my ears had caught the words 'trying to be a hero.' Was that remark just or unjust? I was forced to look into a mirror and examine myself. Perhaps this is why they say that travel broadens the mind. Anyway, I was sore and stayed sore.

The ship sailed soon afterwards and set course for Gibraltar. In the ensuing days I kept to my cabin and occupied myself, over long stretches of time, with reading. I had always been a great reader. This seclusion was owing to the fact that the sight of me still affected some of my fellow-passengers— those with weak intellects—in a certain way. I observed looks, whispers, ripples of amusement. As a young Australian, proud of his manly, independent outlook, I naturally felt huffy about this and even considered shaving off my beard, to provide myself, almost magically, with a new identity (future events were casting shadows before them, as you shall see). However, I decided that would be to take it all too much to heart.

On the fourth day after leaving Naples I went up on deck early in the morning. There was land visible on the port side, far distant, which I knew to be the coast of Morocco. After a while I decided to venture as far forward as possible and, standing by the rail in the bow of the ship and scanning the western horizon, my heart leapt as I saw the Rock of Gibraltar directly ahead. It loomed out of the morning mist. I was the first passenger to spot it.

As I feared, the *Athenic* did not arrive at Southampton on the 10th of August, according to schedule, but on the 12th. Test Matches in those far-off days were three day affairs and the Fifth Test, the final one of the 1902 season, was fixed to take place on the 11th, 12th and 13th. It was clear that the only full day's play it would be possible for me to watch would be the last, and that was disappointing. I was a keen amateur cricketer at home in Australia.

I knew that the result of the series was not in the balance. It would have been better had it been so, but the fact was that the Third and Fourth Tests had been won by Australia, the first two Tests having been drawn. Australia had retained the Ashes.

In the case of the Third Test I had managed to get hold of an English-language newspaper in a Far Eastern port. (I will not say which port as I do not wish to give offence to any nation). The newspaper report of the Third Test, with its odd phraseology, was quite hilarious, and I jotted down one of its sentences in my diary. 'When he was 55 Jessop, the great hitting man, was struck hurtfully on the abdomen and was dismissed by the umpire with ridiculous lbw.' I imagined that if the great English hitter, Gilbert Jessop, had indeed been given out lbw to a ball that struck him in his mid-riff his natural annoyance might have been softened by reading that odd report of the incident.

In the case of the Fourth Test those of us who were cricket enthusiasts received news of it as we steamed westward into the Mediterranean. It may occasion surprise that news was circulated so swiftly in 1902, but to go back fifty years in time is not to go back to beacons burning on hilltops as a means of conveying news. It was the heyday of the telegraph and the pioneer days of the telephone. The world's hunger for news during the Spanish-American War and the Boer War —recently ended—had driven news agencies to criss-cross the wide world with wire and cable.

Any hopes I might have entertained of seeing part of the second day's play at the Oval —perhaps the afternoon session—were dashed when our ship, because of its belated

16

arrival, was forced to dawdle in the vicinity of the Needles, back and forth, for six tedious hours.

I gazed at the famous chalk pinnacles, the stubby, red-topped lighthouse, the pretty, multi-coloured cliffs, and heartily wished to be rid of the sight of them. At long last my wish was granted and we steamed slowly up the Solent and eventually docked.

An hour later I had taken a seat on the London train, sitting opposite a motherly old lady. The train was to start on its journey at any moment. After a while I noticed that the old lady was staring at my face closely, as if she recognised me. I raised my eyebrows and she informed me—some might say solicitously, or some might say officiously—that I had some smuts of soot on my face. Well, I had been to gawp at an incoming locomotive before boarding the London train and I had doubtless ventured too close to it. I smiled weakly and affected an air of indifference. But when I saw her open her bag, take out a handkerchief and moisten it with her tongue I grabbed my valise and fled from the carriage. I was twenty-three years old, not three.

I walked hastily down the platform and heard the guard's whistle and shout. I came abreast of the restaurant car and, seeing a quantity of passengers sitting at a table, made a lightning decision to join them. In those days there was no access from the body of the train to the restaurant car. If you seated yourself there at the start of the journey you remained there. It suited me down to the ground.

The journey began. There was a handsome window to look out of and I was afforded a fine view of the English countryside—woods, meadows, streams and wheatfields. The wheatfields called to mind a favourite hymn:

Fair waved the golden corn
In Canaan's pleasant land,
When full of joy, some shining morn
Went forth the reaper-band.

It was still a little early in the year for the reaper-band, I had to admit. At least, I saw none. I had to admit also that there was not a gum-tree in sight—the trees I cast a professional eye over were all of a dismally low canopy height. England is a land of sun and rain, and so is Gippsland, where I hail from—but there the comparison ends.

A waiter came to my table and stood expectantly and, because I was a little uncertain as to the items on the menu, I ordered coffee and rolls. I knew the journey to London was not a long one and it would not hurt me to fast a little longer.

Later, I noticed, sitting on the other side of the aisle and farther down the car, an elderly man with a magnificent white beard. He had a folded newspaper beside him. I had tried and failed to buy a newspaper at Southampton and I was completely in the dark as to what had happened the day before at the Oval—that is to say, on the first day of the Test Match. I felt I had to satisfy my curiosity and so I rose from my seat, took a few steps down the aisle and stood nervously before the old gentleman.

'Sir, I hope you will excuse me, but I've only today arrived in England. Have you any knowledge of what happened in the Test Match yesterday?'

He stared at me, his eyes blue and watery, and thrust his chin out fiercely. 'Yesterday? Test Match? I'll tell you what happened. Damn Australians batted and made 324, all out. That's what happened.'

I was stung by this and decided to get one thing straight before matters went any further. 'I have the honour, sir, to be an Australian myself.'

'Damn fine fellows, Australians,' he replied, without much softening of his fierceness. 'Always said so. All you colonial chaps pull your weight. Salt of the earth. Damn near as British as we are. Australians the best of the lot. Always said so. We'd never get a decent game of cricket without 'em. Here, take a seat, my boy. Like a good chinwag.'

With a good deal of reluctance I took the

seat opposite him. I had hoped he might offer to lend me the folded newspaper.

'Do you play the game, my boy? You look as if you might be useful.'

I told him I was a member of a small club at home. He went off directly, for he was a talker, not a listener. 'Damned if I'm not myself. Not a small club though. Surrey County Cricket Club. Forty years a member. Only a handful of us old-timers left. Ah, but cricket's not the game it was, you know. I say, those were the days. There was some life in it then. Why, I go back all the way to John Wisden—the 'Little Wonder', as he was nicknamed. He's the fellow who started up the almanack. Do you read it? No, of course, you wouldn't. Great players in those days. There was Parr and Hayward and Carpenter—W.G and his brother, E.M—James Lilleywhite and the Lyttelton brothers—and 'Monkey' Hornby—and what about little Johnny Briggs?'

Was this a question requiring an answer, I wondered. Apparently not, for he was off again. 'Oh, there were one or two useful Australians in those days. What about Spofforth? He could whistle the ball down. He added a bit o' ginger to the proceedings, I can tell you. Tall fellow. Looked as if he were made of india-rubber. Do you know what they called him?' I opened my mouth to answer, but was a shade too late. 'They called him the "Demon Bowler". Nobody remembers his first name, and damned if I can recall it now. Shortish run up to the wicket and over went his arm. Disguised his pace. If he didn't whistle 'em out, he foxed 'em out with his slower one. Held back, you see. No speed merchants like him playing today. This present Australian team's got no speed merchants. Can't call Saunders fast. Batsmen get the best of it today, and why? It's made too easy for 'em. Old W.G still making runs and greybearded. Saw him make 82 a week or two back. Carting the bowling all over the ground. There'll never be another like the Old Man. Game's gone soft. A four-ball over in my day. Now it's six. It's quality we want, not quantity. And what about these declarations? Declaring an innings closed. Never had 'em in my day. We buckled down to it. The batsmen were there to be got out and we got 'em out. That was our way of declaring the innings closed.'

He paused to have a little chuckle. I saw a chance here. 'I think we ought to go back to bowling under-arm, sir.'

This took the old gentleman aback. The little chuckle died in his throat. 'Eh? Bowling under-arm? Oh, I say! What, under-arm? No, no, no, we can't do that. That wouldn't do. But—I say, do you know how over-arm bowling came about? Do you know your cricket history? Do you read Wisden? They say it was a woman—some fellow's sister—who first bowled over-arm. She said she couldn't do otherwise because of her crinoline. She wore a crinoline. Oh, I remember when women wore those things. Good story, but a bit far-fetched, eh?'

He went on with his nostalgic reminiscences, to which I listened with only half an ear. I had heard, at home in my native land, the older generation rhapsodizing about the glories of the past, but I was not impressed. Victor Trumper was my great hero, and I was not to be persuaded that he was in any way inferior to batsmen of yesteryear. In the current series he had showed the English how to bat in the First Test Match with a dashing 104. How I would have loved to have seen that innings.

White Beard had stopped speaking. I saw him looking me up and down. I was just about to thank him for the information he had given me and to get up and return to my seat when he said: 'So you've just arrived here from Aussie-land, eh? Have you a place to go to? Relations or friends?'

I told him I knew nobody in the British Isles. Nobody at all.

'By Jove, you've got some pluck. Come over here to seek your fortune, I suppose,' he said, still eyeing me with his watery, blue eyes.

I only smiled by way of reply.

He told me what I already knew—that London was the largest city in the world—and he added, what I had perhaps not considered, that it was a dangerous city. A lot of 'bad eggs' prowled about railway terminuses. If I were spotted, looking nervously from left to right and wondering in which direction to set off to find a hotel, I might attract the wrong kind of attentions.

He had a niece who ran a small hotel in Marylebone Road. He himself lived in Bayswater and intended to make his way there in a hansom cab. He suggested that I might like to accompany him and he would drop me off at a road junction only a short walk from his niece's hotel.

I gratefully accepted his offer of help.

I shall not attempt to describe my impressions upon arriving at Waterloo Station, beside the River Thames, in the heart of London and hub of the Empire. It was journey's end, and it had been a long journey. At Waterloo Station I simply followed White Beard as if he were my father and I was his small son. Soon I found myself sitting in a hansom cab, lolling contentedly against red velvet cushions, looking all about me with the greatest curiosity.

Glancing upward I could see the tophatted cabbie holding the ribbons in one hand and a long whip in the other. I could see him because our hansom appeared to be a *de luxe* vehicle, having a glass trap. The cab-horse clip-clopped along at a steady pace, with harness jingling.

After a while I turned to White Beard and asked him where were all the trams—the electric ones. I had twice been to Melbourne, and all the wide streets of that city were traversed by new electric trams.

'Trams? Oh, not in Central London. This is Park Lane—the fashionable part of London. That's Hyde Park over there. By Jove, I remember the day I first set foot in Hyde Park. It was in '51. I was twelve years old. Father brought us all up to see the Great Exhibition. The Crystal Palace. Huge building, constructed entirely of glass. Moved it eventually, of course. Still going strong, some-where down in South London. You want to go and stroll in the Park. There's usually a band playing, and there are lots of strange sights.'

'You want me to add to the number?'

My humour, if that is what it was, seemed to confuse him. 'Eh? No, no, no—I mean, a week or two ago I was in the Park and saw a man balancing a big, heavy cart-wheel on his head. Walking along with it perfectly balanced.'

'What was he doing that for?'

'Well, passers-by threw money into his hat on the ground. I threw twopence in.'

(I had heard the English were an eccentric race of people.)

'Ah, I see,' I said. 'Well, I hope he collected enough to buy a headache powder.'

After another period of silence I commented on something I had first noticed at Waterloo Station. 'Everybody seems to wear a hat in London. Straw hats.' I myself was hatless.

'Oh, yes, we all wear boaters in the summer. You must buy a boater, and be in the swim.' Actually, White Beard was not wearing a straw hat but a white, wide-brimmed felt hat. I had to admit it suited him. I did not fancy the idea of a straw hat. I was Australian. I was different, and I intended to remain different.

At last the cab came to a halt at a road junction. It was leave-taking time. I got out of the cab. White Beard pointed out the direction in which I was to walk. 'It's only five minutes walk along there. Bellingham's Private Hotel. Ask for the manageress and say Uncle Bertie sent you. She'll know who Uncle Bertie is. Well, good luck, my boy. I hope you get on all right.'

It was the time for a little speech of thanks, but not the place, with traffic to-ing and fro-ing. I mumbled something. He saw my lips moving—I doubt if he heard what I said—nodded and drew back into the cab. In a moment he was gone and I stood alone on the pavement, holding my valise. My valise was heavy enough, but I was undoubtedly travelling light compared with some of the *Athenic's* passengers I had seen at Southampton, with their several trunks and assorted items of hand luggage.

I gripped my valise and set off along the pavement. Little did I think that inside five minutes I should be precipitated into the strangest adventure ever to befall an overseas visitor to the great metropolis.

CHAPTER TWO

I did not like the look of the sky overhead, for dark clouds were gathering ominously. It would be a cruel blow if the one day's play that remained of the Oval Test Match—which I counted on seeing after a good night's rest—were to be washed out after heavy overnight rain.

Suddenly I spotted a paper-seller on the opposite side of the road and the itch to learn what had been happening at the Oval led me to dash impetuously into the road. I instantly collided with the forequarters of a cab-horse and was thrown heavily to the ground. I heard the whinnying of the horse and a few shouts, but I lay painfully in the grit and dust quite stunned for a minute or two, my wits in a daze. I was not properly sure what had happened to me.

At last I felt myself being hoisted to my feet by a strong pair of arms and, when my feet proved unwilling or unable to support my weight, being carried almost bodily over to the pavement.

'Are you all right, my dear fellow?' I heard somebody say, and when I turned my head I saw a tall man of middle age, dressed in a long travelling coat and with a close-fitting hat on his head of a shape and style I had never seen before. His face was lean and his nose thin and slightly hooked. There was a genuine expression of concern in his deep-set eyes. To allay his fears I smiled weakly and mumbled that I was not hurt. 'Except my legs—a little wobbly.'

His eyes were sharp, however, and he said I had cut the back of my head. The pain I felt in that area told me he was right.

We were standing ringed by a dozen or so bystanders. I looked about for my valise. It was nowhere to be seen. 'Where is my valise?' I said anxiously. A voice from the crowd said: 'I saw a kid run orf with it. The little beggar's pinched it.' This started up a hubbub all round and I looked at Hook Nose rather helplessly. He responded energetically and shepherded me over to the door of the hansom. It dawned on me then that he had been the passenger in the cab when I had run into the horse.

'Anything valuable in it?' he said.

'All my things—a change of clothes...'

'I don't think you will see it again. You had better come with me to my rooms. I feel I have some obligation in the matter.'

A few seconds later I was seated in the hansom and the horse I had collided with— seemingly none the worse for the experience —was being whipped into motion. I felt uneasy, not to say foolish, about what had happened. 'It was my fault entirely,' I said. 'I shouldn't have darted into the road like that. I wanted to buy a newspaper.'

'I doubt if you have your land-legs,' said Hook Nose smoothly, 'so soon after accomplishing a long sea voyage.'

I was puzzled. I could not remember having said anything about—

'How do you know about the sea voyage?'

'Oh, a simple deduction on my part,' said the other casually. 'Your brand of speech—sunburned face—and the smuts on your forehead, which indicate train-travel. You have, out of curiosity, ventured too close to the smoke of the fire-box. Did you, I wonder, arrive at Waterloo from Southampton, or at Fenchurch Street from Tilbury? From Southampton, I would guess. At Tilbury, passenger liners disembark their passengers before noon, more often than not. Ah, I see we are drawing up to the kerb. My rooms are here.'

I decided that my companion in the cab was no ordinary man. He was discerning. He was inquisitive. Yet, was he, in fact, inquisitive? He had asked me no questions. By talking half to himself he seemed to have his own method of getting information from people.

We alighted from the cab and the cabbie

was paid off. As we climbed the stairs to the first floor of the apartment building we had entered, he said: 'Until recently I shared these rooms with an old friend, a widower, a former Army doctor. I miss his company. He is now re-married and setting up a practice in Queen Anne Street, not far from here. I have a housekeeper, Mrs Hudson.'

We stood before a door and he pulled the bell. A minute later a dim light showed through the fanlight, and when I saw the number inscribed thereon I was amazed. It was 221b—a number that instantly brought to mind a memory of the pile of Strand magazines I, regretfully, had had to leave behind in my bookcase. These magazines had devoted many of their pages to the cases of the private detective, Mr Sherlock Holmes, of 221b, Baker Street, in the West End of London.

The door opened and revealed a motherly figure with silvered hair gleaming in the light. 'Ah, Mrs Hudson—you see I am not late back. I have brought with me a young man who has met with a slight accident. Would you be good enough to fetch a bowl of warm water, lint and plaster.'

The realisation that the mysterious stranger I had dubbed Hook Nose was none other than the celebrated Sherlock Holmes had caused me to go weak at the knees. Holmes saw me begin to crumple and put his arm about me. 'Quick, we must get him on to the sofa. He took quite a hard knock.'

Stretched out on a sofa and quite comfortable, the next ten minutes saw me being ministered to by both Holmes and his housekeeper. The one pressed a glass of brandy on me, which wonderfully enlivened me, and the other bathed and dressed my head wound. Holmes then bid the good lady fetch something for us to eat. When she had left the room he elicited from me the admission that I had not so far made any hotel arrangements for the coming night. He insisted that I spend the night in the room recently vacated by his old friend, Doctor Watson. I thanked him and said I would be very glad not to have to stir out of the house and into the gathering dark of the town streets. 'That is settled then,' he said in his brisk manner.

He strode away out of the room and returned a few minutes later dressed in a flowing dressing-gown. He sank himself into his armchair and selected one of the many pipes in his pipe-rack. Now I saw before me one of the Strand magazine illustrations come to life. It was the quintessential Sherlock Holmes, except that, so far as I knew, his mind was not wrestling with some deep problem. And now I saw that he did indeed keep his tobacco in the toe of an old Persian slipper.

'My name is Holmes,' he said succinctly, as he lit his pipe.

'The famous *Sherlock* Holmes?'

He lifted his head and blew a cloud of smoke towards the ceiling. 'Ah, I find you have read some of those narratives my old friend has inflicted upon a long-suffering public. Dear old Watson. Well, I suppose he must be regarded as a man of letters now, as well as a man of medicine.'

'Why don't you write about your cases yourself?'

'I will, my dear young fellow, I will. I propose to devote my declining years to the composition of a textbook which shall focus the whole art of detection into one volume.'

I thought about this for a moment or two. I privately doubted that such a volume, with its inevitable schoolroom flavour, would prove so wonderfully readable as a volume which comprised all of Doctor Watson's narratives.

'Is it one of the highest of the arts?' I asked him.

'The art of detection? It is one of the useful arts. It is not above music.'

As if by magic a violin appeared in his left hand and a bow in his right. They must have been lying on the floor—the room was clean enough but it was untidy. He thrust the violin to his chin and played a snatch of music. When he had done this he asked me: 'Have you ever heard of Paganini?'

'No,' I replied, and added: 'I haven't even heard of Beethoven.'

He subjected me to a long stare.

'I'm a musical ignoramus,' I explained hopelessly.

He laid aside the violin, took up his pipe and puffed at it. After a while he said: 'Paganini played so brilliantly and performed so many technical miracles that many people actually thought he was the Devil incarnate. His appearance, from all accounts, tended to support that notion.'

He stared at me, as if inviting comment. So I responded with: 'I imagine some of the villains you've unmasked have been gripped by that notion—that *you* are the Devil incarnate.'

He digested this. 'Curiously enough, I've not derived so much satisfaction from un-masking villains—and, in some cases, putting them behind bars—as from purely solving a problem. However, some of those villains have been devilish, and, after all, society must be protected. As for myself being regarded as the Devil incarnate, I like to think I am on the side of the angels.'

'Do you know who said that?' This was bold on my part, to play the pedant with the Great Detective, but I was anxious that he should not think I was an all-round ignoramus.

'Said what?'

' "I am on the side of the angels." '

'No—tell me.'

'It was Disraeli in a speech at Oxford. His comment on the Darwin controversy—"Is man an ape or an angel?" '

'Ah, I see I have to deal with a *littérateur*. Enough of this. I now propose to sit back and listen to you, for I believe you have a tale to tell. Who are you and what have you crossed the world in quest of?'

I told him I was John Fairhurst, twenty-three years old, from Bairnsdale, on the Mitchell River, in the state of Victoria, in the Commonwealth of Australia.

'Oh, yes,' said Holmes, 'wasn't it last year you ceased being a colony and became a Commonwealth, and all the states were persuaded to join up together?'

'Federated.'

'Yes—federated. And you have a Prime Minister—and you have a Governor, who acts for the King. Tell me, do you know anybody in England?'

I told him I knew nobody at all in the British Isles. I had spent my working life in forestry and had brought with me an introduction to a man on the Board of Agriculture in London. I hoped to be accepted for a forestry training course at a school which the Government was to start later in the year.

I told him of my love of cricket. I told him of the unexpected diversion of the *Athenic* to Naples. I explained that, because of our late arrival at Southampton, I had been robbed of the chance of being present at the Oval to see all three days of the Fifth Test. 'I plan to go to the Oval tomorrow and see the final day's play.'

Holmes had listened to me with a degree of concentration that was flattering to me.

He was silent for a while. At last he said: 'Cricket is a mystery to me. It is one of the few kinds of mystery with which I have never been inclined to concern myself. Watson is a Great Rugby Football enthusiast. That, too, is a mystery to me. I went in for boxing and fencing at my university—disciplines from which some practical benefit can be derived. Even now, if a young ruffian were to pitch into me I believe I could defend myself pretty well.'

I pointed out that defence was a key element in cricket as well. 'It's no picnic when a fast bowler is—to use your expression—pitching into a batsman.'

'Yes, yes—but the batsman functions in a purely artificial situation. The bowler too. The skills they acquire—and, really, you can acquire a high degree of skill at whittling a stick if you do it every day of the year—the skills they acquire must remain forever unrelated to real life. There is more urgent business to be conducted in life than strutting about in white suits. No, no, no—we shall never agree on this. Watson and I could never agree on it. I could see some sense in it if a man found himself—like the hero chap in Homer—what's-his-name?—being bombarded with rocks by a giant and had to use keen eyesight and agile footwork to save himself from being brained.'

'That conjures up a picture in my mind,' I said. 'I can see the paragraph on the sporting page of the local newspaper. 'Polyphemous, the one-eyed giant, was put on to bowl but, after hurling a few rocks, the umpire ruled that his action was illegal and the captain of the fielding side was instructed to take him off. Polyphemous did not take kindly to this and started hurling rocks at the umpire.'

Holmes chuckled. 'Polyphemous—was that the giant's name? You have read widely. What is more, you are something of a humourist. I might say I envy you that gift. I have sometimes been aware of a lack of humour in my make-up. I doubt if it is something one can cultivate.'

Mrs Hudson arrived to spread a tablecloth over the table and serve us with a supper of chops and vegetables. I cleared my plate without difficulty, for I had not eaten anything substantial for over six hours.

Over the meal Holmes said that he had been returning from a visit to a doctor when I had my undignified brush with the cab-horse. His health had not been good of late and he had been ordered to take life more easily. I studied his lean face and it certainly lacked colour. I also thought I detected a trembling in his sinewy hands.

'London is far from being the healthiest of cities to live in,' he observed. 'The fogs in winter kill people off by the thousand.'

'I've heard about your fogs,' I said. 'Does your friend, Doctor Watson, know that you are not in the best of health?'

'It would not do for him to know—he would fuss and worry. He is only two weeks back from his honeymoon and is occupied with fitting himself out in his new domicile. He is renting two floors of a large house in Queen Anne Street.'

'Which—I believe you said—is not far from here.'

'Five minutes walk. I went round to see him a day or two ago and he had just had his brass plates put up. He had been in practice before, of course.'

'An Army doctor, you said.'

'Yes—although his experience of Army life was short. He saw action in the Second Afghan War and stopped a bullet. On top of that he went down with a nasty bout of fever. He was invalided out of the service, came back to England and, soon afterwards, we met.'

We continued our conversation for an hour or so after supper, but eventually my eyelids began to droop—a symptom not likely to have escaped the notice of such as Sherlock Holmes. He rose to his feet and said he would show me my room.

'You are bent upon watching your cricket match tomorrow then?'

I nodded, smiling apologetically.

'You would not prefer,' he continued, 'a stroll among the streets and back-alleys of Limehouse or Wapping—spying out the haunts of petty thieves and opium eaters? I have plenty of old clothes in a trunk that I make use of for disguise purposes.'

I said I should prefer to be at the Oval. However, when he opened a window and I heard the sound of heavy rain beating on the street below, I groaned. He shut the window and said: 'We have had a surfeit of this sort of thing this year. I bid you goodnight. We will breakfast at nine o'clock.'

As I lay in bed I had to endure the queasy, floating sensation inevitably experienced by the sea voyager when first attempting to sleep on terra firma after forty-five nights on the rolling bosom of the ocean. However, when I did fall asleep I slept soundly enough.

CHAPTER THREE

At a quarter past ten the following morning I stood poised and ready to leave No 221b, Baker Street—to hire a hansom to take me back across London the way I had come the day before, and on to the Kennington Oval. It was not raining and patches of blue sky were in evidence. Yet I have to record that, shortly afterwards, something occurred which caused me to postpone my departure. What was it that brought about this fateful change of plan?

I rose a full hour before breakfast, and before Holmes stirred, and sat comfortably in the sitting-room. Soon the admirable Mrs Hudson brought me a cup of tea and the *Times* newspaper, and I leapt to read the account of the previous day's play. On the first day Australia had indeed batted all day and made 324, just as White Beard had said. Beyond that bald statistic the paper told me nothing except that Hugh Trumble, the off-break bowler, had been top scorer with 64 to his credit. I was left to wonder what sort of first innings score Victor Trumper had achieved. I glanced about but could not see a copy of yesterday's *Times* anywhere—it was doubtless in the housekeeper's room and I did not like to trouble her for it.

I then settled in to read the full account given of the second day's play and it seemed that England had had to bat on a rain-affected pitch, difficult to score runs on. As in Australia's innings the most useful knock had been achieved by a bowler—in England's case, the Yorkshireman, George Hirst—who had scraped up an invaluable 43. England saved the dreaded follow-on after some anxious moments and struggled to 183. Trumble had taken 8 for 65 with his off-breaks.

So Australia began their second innings and my heart sank as I read, for Victor

Trumper had been brilliantly run out to the fielding of Gilbert Jessop. Trumper's wicket was, unquestionably, the prize scalp for the home side and, greatly heartened, they had pressed hard, with the result that at close of play Australia had lost 8 wickets for a meagre 114 runs. The feeling was that England were not yet out of it, and everything pointed to an exciting last day's play, if the weather held.

Holmes at last appeared and we enjoyed a breakfast of smoked haddock, a fish new to me which I thought quite delicious. After the meal the quarter was softly chimed by the clock on the mantelpiece. I had no packing to do, not having a valise, and, I repeat, I was poised and ready to leave, feeling a little awkward, as one does when one is leave-taking. Suddenly Mrs Hudson entered and told Holmes that there was a caller on the telephone for him. I was somewhat surprised to learn that he owned a telephone; apparently (as I later learned) it was installed in the passageway close by Mrs Hudson's room, its ringing, therefore, within earshot of that good lady but unheard—mercifully, I imagine—by Holmes. He went off to attend to the call and I was left glancing at the clock and thinking that I must not dilly-dally or I should leave myself too little time to make the journey to the Oval. I did not want to miss any of the play.

When Holmes returned his brow was puckered. 'My dear Fairhurst, here is one of the oddest coincidences I have ever run across. Here are you, my unexpected overnight guest, about to set off to the Kennington Oval for the Test Match, and I have just received a call from a peer of the realm, a certain Lord Hawke, whom I confess to never having heard of. He claims to be the Chairman of the England Test Match Selection Board and he wishes to call upon me and consult me about what he describes as ''a very serious matter.'' Leaving aside my settled conviction that nothing that has to do with the game of cricket could, justifiably, be described as 'very serious', what am I to make of it? He is bringing with him another gentleman, the Secretary of the Surrey Cricket Club—thus I presume it has something to do with the current Test Match. The pair of them will be here in ten minutes or so.'

All I could say was: 'It's unbelievable. Of course, I believe what you say, but—'

Holmes chuckled. 'Even I find it hard to believe, and I am accustomed to out-of-the-ordinary occurrences. My dear fellow, you must not think of departing just yet.'

'Oh, but if I don't go now I shall miss—'

'Half an hour will not make any difference, surely, I am so used to having Watson beside me during interviews of this kind, acting as a sort of counterweight to the client. You must also consider my poor understanding of anything that pertains to the mystery of cricket. I should take it as a great favour if you would hold off going for an hour or so.'

I did not fail to notice that 'half an hour' had become elongated to 'an hour or so'.

Nevertheless, I agreed to postpone my departure. He had been exceptionally kind to me and, besides, I had missed the chance of seeing Trumper batting in a Test Match on English soil. I, however, confessed myself nervous of the prospect of being in the presence of a member of the aristocracy.

'Pooh!' said Holmes dismissively. 'That is not the proper Bohemian spirit. One should not be intimidated by titles. My philosophy is that if a man struts about in a tall, silk hat, what is it but a provocation to some corner-boy to knock it off? No need to be nervous. In any event, you will merely be holding a watching brief. I scent an interesting case, my boy. My instinct in these matters is seldom wrong. I must go and change into more suitable attire.'

He retired into his bedroom and came back a few minutes later and strode to the window. He peered down at the street below. 'Ha! A cab is drawing up to the kerb. Two men are alighting. Our visitors are here on cue. The blood is quickening in my veins.' He went to stand with his back to the small fire in the grate, rubbing his hands and smiling with the pleasure of anticipation.

'Do you think it wise,' I said diffidently, 'to involve yourself in a case. By your own admission, you are not a well man. Your doctor said—'

'Oh, a doctor's advice cannot be slavishly followed. It is true he advised me to go carefully, but my mind rebels against stagnation. Give me a problem to solve and my health will mend in the solving of it. I abhor the dull routine of existence. Besides, I have enlisted you—with your kind acquiescence— as a replacement for my old friend, Watson, and you must do as he used to do—lay a restraining hand on me at times when I act too impetuously.'

'I thought *I* was the one who was in the habit of acting impetuously, Mr Holmes. Remember my dash into the street?'

'Indeed I do, and I am relieved to notice that you do not seem to be suffering any ill-consequences this morning. What a thing is the resilience of youth!'

The door opened, following a light tap, and Mrs Hudson ushered in two men. One, who led the way, was not tall, but strongly and squarely built; his moustache was full, but it had been trimmed to keep it from bushiness, and I was beginning to learn that this was the fashion of the day. The other man was a generation older and he was inclined to a paunch and his moustache was silver-streaked and straggling. 'Mr Sherlock Holmes?' began the younger man in a forthright voice, with a touch of hauteur in it; he eyed the owner of that name and I received not the tithe part of a glance.

'At your service, my lord,' returned Holmes crisply.

'We spoke on the telephone, which is a tiresome instrument, but useful. Is my name known to you, Mr Holmes?'

'I have to confess that I had not heard your name before.'

'Indeed, that is most surprising,' said his

lordship, raising his eyebrows. 'My name is a household word in cricketing circles.'

'Ah, but you see, I have never revolved in cricketing circles,' said Holmes, quite unabashed.

Lord Hawke cleared his throat and let his eyes rove about the room. He could not have failed to notice its general untidiness and he blinked when he saw a sheaf of correspondence and bills lying on a writing-desk and transfixed by a wicked-looking knife. I saw the thought framed in his eyes—was Mr Sherlock Holmes a gentleman?

'Shall we come to the "very serious matter" you spoke of on the telephone?' said Holmes.

'Yes, yes, of course. Time is pressing. Mr Holmes, I am here in London in my capacity as Chairman of the Test Match Selection Board, but my ordinary sphere of activities is in the city of Leeds, the headquarters of Yorkshire cricket. Sir, not to waste words, I *am* Yorkshire cricket. You will search in vain, north or south of the river Trent, for anyone willing or able to challenge that statement. Now this matter concerns a member of the England team engaged in the Oval Test Match. He is Wilfred Rhodes, a Yorkshire professional—a young man I have had under my wing for some time. He is nothing short of a cricketing prodigy, a fine all-rounder and, I venture to prophesy, a rising star of the very greatest magnitude.'

'Indeed, that is high praise,' said Holmes lazily, and suggested: 'A future England captain perhaps.'

'A future England captain!' echoed his lordship in a tone of sharp indignation. 'What do you mean? Rhodes is a professional cricketer—I thought I had made that quite clear. Pray heaven the day will never come when a professional captains England!'

'Why, what would be objectionable in that?'

'My dear sir, what is required of a captain is firm, fearless leadership. Men in the lower walks of life will never obey, readily or wholeheartedly, one of their own fellows.'

'Ah, I see,' said Holmes. 'Now, concerning Wilfred Rhodes—'

'Yes, yes—I must relate the sequence of events as they occurred this morning. Rhodes and George Hirst, his Yorkshire and England colleague, travel by train down to London several times a season for Test Matches and county matches and habitually lodge at a boarding-house in Eversley Gardens, a residential road on the south side of the Euston Road. It is convenient because it is within walking distance of St Pancras Station, the terminus at which they arrive and from which they depart when they have played their matches. This morning Hirst came down to breakfast at eight o'clock and at half past eight Rhodes had not put in an appearance. A maid reported that he was not in his room and that the door of his room was ajar. At nine o'clock, in accordance with the timetable to which the two cricketers always strictly adhere, Hirst left for the Oval. He was puzzled and worried, for one of the boarders had said that he had heard a noise on the landing at about half-past four in the morning, as of a man gasping and groaning. He had peeped out, seen no-one, but noticed that Rhodes' door was ajar. It seemed to Hirst, therefore, that his colleague had quitted his room, and presumably the house also, at the unaccountably early hour of half-past four—a full hour before dawn light.'

'Had quitted it,' said Holmes, thoughtfully, 'or, perhaps been forcibly removed from it. Was a search made in the house and over the grounds?'

'Yes, indeed—a thorough search. The landlady was anxious about her lodger's strange disappearance, from the point of view of not wanting any adverse publicity. She well understood his celebrity as a sportsman. When Hirst arrived at the Oval he straightway reported the affair to Mr Alcock here, the Secretary of the Surrey club. While they were discussing it in his office a very surprising thing happened—a steward brought in a note which had been thrust into his hand by an anonymous urchin. After looking at it he immediately took a cab to my rooms in Jermyn Street, where I stay when I am in London.'

'I presume the note was folded, as notes usually are,' said Holmes.

Mr Alcock spoke now for the first time. 'Yes, it was folded several times, with one part tucked, like a flap, into the other part.'

'I think I know the method,' said Holmes. 'And was the urchin inside the ground when he gave the note to the steward?'

'No, no—the steward was helping to prepare the turnstile positions when the boy approached him, thrust the note at him, saying: "For Mr Alcock"—and scampered away.'

'Ah, he said that, did he?—that is most interesting.'

Lord Hawke cleared his throat and took up the tale. 'At my rooms I was entertaining Sir George Barkworth, an old friend of mine, to breakfast, and we all three discussed the note. It was Sir George who suggested I get in touch with you, Mr Holmes. In his address book he had your telephone number which, I understand, you do not circulate indiscriminately. You are acquainted with Sir George, I believe.'

'Yes,' said Holmes. 'I helped to clear up a little mystery at his country house last October. A young blackmailer was brought to book. During the investigation I believe I did give him my number. I had just at that time had a telephone installed here.'

'Here is the note,' said Lord Hawke. 'As you will see, the message comprises only eleven words.' As he gave the note to Holmes I edged in close beside him, being curious to see it myself. He immediately introduced me as his young assistant, privy to all his secrets—a blatant untruth, but a kindly and paternal gesture, I thought. I did not look over his shoulder so much as round it, he being six or seven inches taller than me.

The eleven words had clearly been scissored from some printed matter and stuck on a nondescript slip of paper. They read:

sahib cricketer in good hands pray the Italian will keep alive.

'The words are from a magazine, are they not?' said Lord Hawke.

'Or cut out of a dictionary,' said Mr Alcock.

Holmes shot him a keen glance. 'A dictionary is an astute guess. Not a kindly way to treat a useful work of reference, but the quickest, surest method of finding words—a method I might have employed myself. However, I believe they have not been cut from a dictionary, but from a thesaurus, for where is the accenting and syllabication that words in a dictionary invariably show? Now it is not every man who keeps a thesaurus on his bookshelf. A professional man does. He will have acquired it during his student days. A student treasures his Roget when he is working up to his professional examinations, but he casts it aside when the need to write theses and such things is behind him, and he would think little of mutilating it if it served his purpose.'

'You think there is a professional man behind this mystery?' said Lord Hawke.

'It is only a theory,' replied Holmes dryly. 'One must start somewhere. There are deep waters in this message.'

'You say, "if it served his purpose"—but what can be his purpose? The message succeeds only in mystifying. What can it mean?'

'It is mystifying, I agree,' said Holmes. 'And, of course, knowing how the words have been assembled—cut from a thesaurus —does not help much, except that, if we were later to discover that there had been foul play, and the malefactor were to be arrested on suspicion, he would stand condemned if it were found that a thesaurus in his possession had these eleven words cut from it.'

'That word "sahib," Mr Holmes—'said Mr Alcock—'do you think that points to an Indian having sent the note? And the word "Italian"—do you think the Zenucci gang might somehow be involved?'

Holmes smiled. 'The members of the

Zenucci gang are all illiterate—or so my old friend, Inspector Lestrade, informs me.'

'Mr Holmes,' cut in Lord Hawke impatiently. 'Mr Alcock has arranged to telephone his assistant at the Oval at eleven o'clock, and I see it is eleven o'clock now. We must find out if Rhodes has appeared at the ground. Play begins at half-past eleven, but there is a strict rule that players must have reported to the team captain by eleven at the very latest. If Rhodes has not reported I feel there must be something seriously wrong, and I shall ask you if you would be willing to undertake an investigation of the affair. I shall, of course, eventually have to notify the police, but I propose to take it upon myself to hold off that course of action for a while. May we use your telephone?'

'Certainly, my lord,' said Holmes. 'But first, one thing. If you call upon my services, then, whatever the outcome, no fee is to be involved. No retainer, honorarium —no requital of any kind. Is that understood?'

Lord Hawke hesitated, but answered: 'As you wish.'

'Will you come this way,' said Holmes, and led the two visitors out of the room.

CHAPTER FOUR

Holmes had placed the mysterious message on the table, and I felt that, as his "young assistant", I was entitled to take it up and study it—not that my study yielded anything that went beyond what Holmes had offered as conjecture. The wording was indeed enigmatic, but should it be interpreted as sinister or threatening? Had something fearful happened to Wilfred Rhodes—or was there a perfectly bland explanation?

I went to the window but could not see a great deal of the sky, and it was not easy to determine whether the clouds were high or low. My attention was caught by a small framed photograph on the wall, of a woman not without some pretensions to beauty. Her signature, in faded ink, was scrawled at the bottom and read: Irene Adler.

Then I saw a walking-stick lying behind Holmes' chair. It was what we called a knob-stick, and I picked it up. In my imagination I pictured the scene at the Oval cricket ground where cricket-lovers—people from all walks of life—were passing through the turn-stiles and taking up the favoured positions on seats and benches. I pictured, too, the scene in the England dressing-room where players were lacing up their boots, eager to get out onto the field and go for the quick capture of the two remaining Australian wickets. Was the team, inexplicably, a man short?

The feel of the knobstick in my hands led me into a whimsical reverie—a fantasy in which I had come in at No 11 with Australia needing four to win both the match and the series, and the last ball of the day to be bowled. I saw the England pace bowler charge up to the wicket, his legs a flurry of white trouser, a ferocious snarl on his lips. Over went his arm. Overpitched! The knobstick cut through the still, stale air of the sitting-room and, in my imagination, the final ball of the final Test Match went speeding sweetly to the boundary, and deep extra cover, with a flip of his head, could only sink to his knees in despair.

I rehearsed the drive half a dozen times, but when I heard a buzz of voices out on the landing I hurriedly put the knobstick back where I had found it. I heard the front door close a minute or two later and then, after a quick patter of feet on the stairs, Holmes entered the room with a photograph in his hand. He was looking grim but not displeased.

'Well, my dear Fairhurst, here is a pretty puzzle. ''The Case of the Missing No 11'', as Doctor Watson would most likely call it. No 11, I am given to understand, is the number in the batting order at which Rhodes goes in to bat. Or does *not* go in to bat, as it may turn out.' He put the photograph face downwards on the table and took up the mysterious note. He moved over to the fireplace, stood with his back to the mantelpiece and stared hard at the note for several minutes. The room was silent except for the ticking of the clock, and I dared not interrupt his train of thought.

Suddenly he lifted his head and his eyes seemed to blaze in their dark sockets.

Now I spoke. 'Is there no sign of him at the Oval then?'

He shot me a glance. 'No, but I have a shrewd idea where we shall find him, and I am a good deal uneasy concerning the situation we shall find him in.'

He went to the table and handed me the photograph. 'This is our man. His teammate, Hirst, furnished Lord Hawke with it. Rhodes is the smaller of the two men.'

There were, as Holmes indicated, two men in the photograph, and the man I took to be Rhodes, smaller in stature and younger in years, had a plain, oval-shaped face with a modest expression in the eyes and a quietly determined set of the mouth. He wore one of the well-trimmed moustaches, fashionable among young men of that day.

'You think you know where—but you've no clues as to where he is, surely,' I said.

He had reached for a heavy directory—one of several that stood in a row on the top shelf of his bookcase—and was swiftly turning over pages. 'No clues indeed! I believe we have. I believe one of those eleven words on the note provides a most promising clue. Ah, here we are. Yes—well, that is no great distance from Baker Street, but too far to walk. Energy must be conserved.' He replaced the directory on the bookshelf. He turned to me. 'My boy, I know I can depend on you to lend me your assistance for an hour or two.' He saw, I imagine, signs of dismay and alarm in my eyes. 'Now I put it to you. Would you really insist upon running off to a cricket match when I offer you the opportunity of helping me to investigate a mystery, the unravelling of which may, for all we know at this stage, result in the saving of a man's life? A cricketer's life, what is more. You would not turn your back on that, would you?'

When he put it like that, what could I do but smile wanly and assure him that I would be glad to go along with him and render him all possible assistance. 'I'm bound to say, Mr Holmes, that you've been very good to me—'

'Oh, nonsense—it's not really benevolence on my part. I dare say I want your company for good, practical reasons. Doctor Watson and I have set off from this room I don't know how often, pursuing some hopeful line of enquiry, and there have been times when I have asked my old friend to slip his Army revolver in his pocket. Now, in the generality of cases I happen to think a strong pair of shoulders will serve as well in a tight corner. You, I see, are not ill-equipped in that department, and neither are you wanting in native intelligence. Well?'

Five minutes later we were sitting in a hansom and wheeling away from No 221b, Baker Street. I had no notion where we were going, whether north, east, south or west, and no inkling as to our destination. I had, reluctantly, agreed to throw my shoulders and native intelligence into the pool of our combined resources and—I had to admit it now—was beginning to feel a little tingle of excitement.

Holmes bent his dark, saturnine face close to mine and spoke with peculiar force. 'Remember the eleven words of the message: *sahib cricketer in good hands pray the Italian will keep alive.* Viewed as a whole it presents three mysteries. Who sent it? Why was it sent? Why is it phrased in so cryptic a form? It may be that we shall solve the first two mysteries by getting to the bottom of the third. Presumably it is cryptic because it is designed to deceive. We must not be deceived. The enemy, and I speak in military terms, positions himself upon a hill—a vantage point—from which he is able to look down upon us. What we have to do is to dislodge him from that vantage point, so that *we* may look down upon *him.*'

'In that message,' I said hesitantly. 'Are you saying that he has shown his hand?'

'I believe he has shown a corner of it,' said Holmes. He peered out of the cab window. 'We are turning into Oxford Street. The racket will prevent conversation.'

Sure enough, we turned to the left and the traffic noise escalated dramatically. I had never heard of Oxford Street but I was willing to believe it was one of the main arteries through London. The noise was thunderous, with jarveys shouting, whips cracking and hooves stamping and ringing on the roadway. Holmes sat back with eyes closed, rapt in thought, oblivious to the hurly-burly all about him. When, much later, we had turned away from the main stream of traffic and the noise-level had dropped appreciably, he seemed to come to himself, like a man recovering from a fainting fit, and opened his eyes. He glanced keenly at me. Perhaps he wondered if my mind were upon the matter in hand, or wandering south of the Thames.

'Two of the eleven words in the message

stand out as probably having a special significance. What two words, do you think?'

I went over the words in my mind. I had memorised them. I pondered for a while and then suggested the words 'sahib' and 'Italian'.

'I would not disagree,' said Holmes, and I could not help feeling flattered. 'The word ''sahib'' is perhaps the more interesting of the two but it must be set aside for the moment. The word ''Italian'' is the one which we are to deal with quite soon, and I believe it may provide a good foothold as we begin to climb the hill of this mystery.' A little while later he said: 'To test your powers of observation, listen and tell me what you hear. Listen!'

Obediently I listened. All I could hear at first was the measured clip-clop of the horse's hooves and the harsh, grating sound of the wheels on the roadway. Visibility was restricted when sitting back comfortably in a hansom and so I was not tempted to use my eyes. Suddenly I noticed a different sound that could only be a difference in the surface of the road. I was aware that the cab's wheels were running more smoothly and quietly. After a while the old grating sound returned. I turned to Holmes and remarked on this.

'Yes,' he said. 'The road surface was smoother there for a distance of about a hundred yards. How would you explain that?'

'Well, I think that section is paved differently.'

'You are right. It is paved with wood-blocks. For what reason, do you think?'

'To reduce the noise of passing traffic.'

'And who, in particular, would wish the noise to be reduced?'

'Well, the first thing that springs to mind is a church. The parson likes to hear himself speak when he's reading the lesson.'

'Church, yes. Anything else spring to mind?'

I had to think for a while before coming up with a suggestion: 'A hospital. What about a hospital?'

'Good! Your thinking is clear-headed and your conclusions are expressed with admirable terseness. In fact, that was a church we passed—St George's in Bloomsbury Way—but, as you say, a section of the road outside a hospital would also be laid with woodblocks to muffle the noise of traffic. Tell me, my dear Fairhurst—have you ever, in your short life, been taken ill and confined to a hospital?'

I must say that I was not a little bewildered by the drift of the questioning, which seemed to have swung wildly over to my medical history, but I answered tamely: 'As a matter of fact, I have. When I was twelve years old I went down with diphtheria and was laid up for two weeks in Bairnsdale Hospital.'

'Indeed?' said Holmes. 'That is most interesting.'

'It was touch and go with me,' I continued. 'Of course, our hospital isn't a grand building—Bairnsdale being only a small place. I don't suppose it had as many as a dozen beds. Yes, I was pretty ill.'

'Diphtheria is a nasty business. Your mother and father were anxious then? There was cause for anxiety?'

'Oh, you can be sure of that.'

'Nevertheless,' Holmes persisted, 'when you had been taken to the hospital—despite the fact that it was not a grand building, they were confident you were in good hands, eh?'

'I dare say they were.' What was he rambling on about, I wondered. Had he said that the word 'Italian' provided a clue to the mystery of Wilfred Rhodes? Was he all right? Had his weakness gone to his head? The sky is getting darker, I thought, and so is all the questioning.

Five minutes elapsed. I wondered if that were the end of it. Suddenly he spoke again. 'Your mother and father paid many a visit to the hospital to learn of your progress, I have no doubt. Nevertheless, as you have confirmed to me, they both were thankful that you were *in good hands*, and they trusted that the doctors and nurses would *keep alive*

75

their fever-ridden son. Is that right?'

A thrill surged through me as I recognised the two phrases he had emphasised. The eleven words of the cryptic message ran through my mind: *sahib cricketer in good hands pray the Italian will keep alive.*

'Listen!' said Holmes urgently. Once again, listening, I detected the transition from the harsh, grating noise of the wheels to a quieter sound. Holmes tapped on the trap-door above him and it lifted off, showing the face of the cabbie. 'Stop here, cabbie.'

Holmes climbed out of the cab and I followed, immediately becoming aware that a fine rain was falling. We had stopped at one end of a small square; to the left there was a small hedged-round park area, and I could see a nanny hurriedly pushing a perambulator and seeking shelter from the rain; to the right a tall white building claimed my notice. It was clearly a very new building, of four storeys and elegant design; entrance to it was through a central Roman arch.

·Inscribed boldly on the front of it were the words OSPIDALE ITALIANO—and it did not require a profound knowledge of Italian to be able to translate that.

So, I thought, the word *Italian* refers to this hospital, according to Holmes' theory, and he expects to find the missing cricketer in this building. We were, indeed, on the threshold of an intriguing adventure. I glanced at him admiringly. 'Bravo, Mr Holmes—you have dislodged the enemy from his vantage point, just as you said.'

He shook his head vigorously. 'No, no—it is too soon to say that.' He took his watch from his pocket and looked at it thoughtfully, and I saw his fingers close upon a bright sovereign that was held by a link to his watch-chain. He turned to me, saying, rather wistfully: 'You see this sovereign—it was given to me by a woman whose name was Irene Adler. She was, by profession, an opera singer, although some would have described her as an adventuress. Perhaps you noticed her photograph on the wall at

Baker Street. Perhaps you wondered at it. My dear Fairhurst, I had not thought a woman capable of outwitting me, but that is what she did. She outwitted me. I shudder to think of it. Watson has written his account of what happened in a tale he calls ''A Scandal in Bohemia''. I shall never become too sure of myself while I have this sovereign on my chain. It serves as a salutary reminder that Sherlock Holmes himself is not infallible.'

He seemed to jerk his mind back to present business, for he thrust his watch back into his pocket and buttoned his coat with purposeful vigour. He bade the cabbie to await our return and said to me: 'Come— we must put it to the test. Do not look surprised by anything I say to you when we are inside. We are about to practise a little innocent deception within the next half-hour.'

As we walked across the square I asked him why there should be an Italian Hospital in the heart of London. 'You are probably not aware,' he said, 'that many thousands of Italians work in London, chiefly in the hotel and restaurant business. There are also legions of organ-grinders and vendors— sellers of hokey-pokey, as I believe they call it.'

'Hokey-pokey? What in the world's that?'

'Some kind of frozen watery confection. I've not sampled it myself.'

We passed boldly into the hospital, under the Roman arch, and approached the reception desk. It was presided over by a stout, middle-aged lady, dressed in a dark green uniform and wearing a white cap, fastened by strings under her ample chin.

Holmes bowed to her. '*Signora, buon giorno. Come sta lei?*'

'*Molto bene, grazie,*' answered the lady quietly and without smiling.

'I regret I cannot continue to address you in your beautiful language—the language spoken by Corelli, Albinoni, Tartini, Paganini—'

The lady arched her eyebrows and, still

without a change of expression, said: 'Will you please state your business.'

'*Signora,*' said Holmes, placing a hand lightly on my shoulder, 'this gentleman is Mr John Rhodes, whose brother, Wilfred, has been missing since early this morning, and we have reason to believe that he may have met with an accident of some kind. My young friend's brother was staying at a boarding-house not far from here—.' He stopped speaking. It was clear from the expression on the receptionist's face that she knew something about the mystery; she had bent her head and was poring over a thick book which lay open before her.

She looked up. '*Signor,* a young man was brought to the hospital this morning at twenty-five minutes past five. I was not myself on duty at that time but I have a record of his admission here. I think I must take you to see Doctor Bartoli who is dealing with the case.' She beckoned to another uniformed lady sitting at a table in the rear and when that lady approached the reception desk she spoke a few mellifluous words of Italian to her. Then she led Holmes and I out of the hall, down a corridor to a door at the end.

A minute or two later we stood in Doctor Bartoli's office. He was a small, squat man with a black beard and thick spectacles. Holmes introduced himself and me by saying: 'My name is Holmes, and this is Mr John Rhodes.'

The doctor's eyes lit up. 'Ah, so your name is Holmes, is it? I have often wondered who you were.'

Holmes frowned. 'We have met previously, doctor?'

'No, no, do not mistake me. We have not met, but I have seen you many times.'

'In Baker Street? You live in that corner of London?'

'No, no, I have seen you promenading. Promenading. Does that enlighten you?'

'Ah, so you have noticed me at the Queen's Hall. At the Henry Wood Promenade Concerts.'

'Oh, yes, many times. You will forgive me for saying you have a striking appearance. However, to business, Mr Holmes.' He rose from his chair and came round his desk to stand before me and stare at me intently for a few moments. 'Yes, I see it clearly—the family likeness of your young friend to his brother.'

'He is here then?' said Holmes. 'Is he seriously ill?'

Before answering the doctor returned to his desk and sat down. 'Perhaps I had better tell you what occurred. The unfortunate young man was brought to this hospital in a hansom cab. He was in a coma. Molinari, one of our porters, put the patient on a trolley-on-wheels and took him to the casualty station where I was on hand to examine and treat him. His lips and skin were livid in colour and there was a cold sweat on his skin. The pupils of his eyes were like pinpoints. I decided that he had been injected with something that had had a toxic effect—perhaps a drug, in itself toxic, or, perhaps, a massive overdose of a non-toxic drug. His respiration was depressed—dangerously so—and I immediately gave oxygen. You have to consider, Mr Holmes, that I was not sure whether I had not to deal with one of these poor, weak-willed creatures who have become addicted to opiates and are in the habit of injecting themselves....'

'Yes, yes, of course,' Holmes broke in, brusquely. 'But I must tell you that that can be ruled out. Mr Rhodes is a very uncomplicated man. He is a very physically active man. A sportsman.'

'I did rule it out, Mr Holmes, when I found only one puncture in his skin. It did not require the acute intelligence of a Sherlock Holmes to conclude that the patient was not...'

He stopped speaking abruptly, leaving the sentence unfinished. He stared hard at Holmes and I heard him utter some exclamation in his own language.

Holmes broke the awkward silence by saying: 'You seem to have penetrated my disguise, doctor. The disguise of no disguise. It has sometimes proved effective, but not, it would appear, on this occasion.'

'You are the famous detective, Sherlock Holmes, of Baker Street?' said the doctor, deeply impressed.

'I cannot deny it,' said Holmes, relaxing his features into a smile. 'You had not, perhaps, associated the man you have seen, standing rapt at the Queen's Hall, listening to Beethoven's "Missa Solemnis", with the unhallowed activities of criminal investigation. Well, this puts the interview on a different footing. I must be frank with you. I have to tell you that I have been asked to investigate the mystery surrounding your young patient—his movements in the early hours of this morning and the strange manner of his arrival at your hospital. Is he dangerously ill, can you tell me?'

'He has been dangerously ill, yes, Mr Holmes, and his condition still gives cause for concern—but he is clearly a young man in superb physical shape and, therefore, I confidently expect him to make a rapid recovery once the toxic elements in his system have been eliminated.' To my surprise he suddenly turned to me. 'You will be relieved to hear me say that, Mr Rhodes.'

I had to think quickly. Holmes stood revealed in his true identity, but who was I? Was I still John Rhodes, the anxious brother of the patient? Although I did not then know it, for the remainder of that day I was to be the leading actor in an extraordinary, and sometimes quite comical, drama of false identity—and this was to be the curtain-raiser to it.

I decided not to drop my mask. 'Yes, doctor—relieved.' I spoke softly and uttered as few words as seemed needful.

The doctor turned back to Holmes. 'You suspect foul play perhaps. I was of the opinion, from the manner of his arrival here, that the circumstances were suspicious.'

'He was brought here in a hansom, you say,' said Holmes. 'The cab-driver—can you describe him? Had he any distinguishing features?'

'Well, I did not see him myself, but Molinari, the porter, did mention that he had *capelli rossi*—red hair. I can have Molinari come here to my office, if you wish.'

'I don't think that will be necessary,' said Holmes. 'Did the cabbie say anything to him, do you know?'

'Very little. He merely said the unconscious man was ill and needed treatment. That was obvious in any case. He did not linger a second longer than it took to get the sick man out of the cab and on to a trolley. He went off in great haste. That, I think, is suspicious in itself.'

Holmes, while the doctor had been speaking, had unbuttoned his coat, taken out his watch and consulted it. 'Doctor, I am grateful to you for your frankness. I have a line of enquiry to follow elsewhere and time is pressing. Your time is valuable too. I would like to get in touch with you later in the day. I bid you good morning.'

We made a swift exit from the doctor's room and from the hospital. Once in the open air we found that our cabbie had moved his cab across the square to a horse trough; the horse stood quietly and contentedly having, presumably, long since slaked his thirst. As we came up I was amused to read an inscription on the side of the trough: NEW DAYS, NEW WAYS— THESE PASS, LOVE STAYS. I was struck by the incongruity of a sentimental verse inscribed on so inglorious an item of street furniture.

Holmes, without preamble, enquired of our man if he knew of a fellow-cabbie with ginger or auburn hair.

'Well, guv—let's think. There's Ginger Moxon, he's cabbying round this district. He's one o' Dashwood's men. Dashwood's a big cab proprietor over by King's Cross Station.'

'Do you think you could find him?'

'Well, the station's the best place to look for him. He might be on the rank there. O' course, on the other 'and, he might be at the cab-shelter—we all knock off for a cup o' tea and a bun between twelve and one. What's the matter, guv—has Ginger been up to no good?'

'What would you say of his character?' said Holmes.

The cabbie grinned. 'Oh, Ginger's all right, guv. He's a bit of a fly boy though. He'd do anything for an extra shilling.' His grin broadened. 'Same as I would, guv.'

'King's Cross Station,' said Holmes, and we took our seats. The cab bounced as the cabbie leapt up, the whip cracked and we set off.

'Well, my boy,' said Holmes, sinking back into the cushions, 'you played your part splendidly. You judged the situation to a nicety. I cut the interview short, you will have noticed. For the time being the good doctor remains in ignorance as to the patient's precise identity, and it is better he should. It is better that nothing should leak out to the newspapers. It might hamper our investigation.'

'I've not had a chance to look at English newspapers,' I remarked. 'Only the sports page of the *Times* this morning, before breakfast.'

'A mixed bag. There was a time when reports of scandals and nefarious activities were meat and drink to me and I never tired of reading the more sensational papers. That, of course, was when I was qualifying myself for my profession and accumulating a store of knowledge that I could draw on for my own peculiar purposes. I owe newspapers a great deal and it would be churlish of me to gird at them now that I am in the sunset of my career and I do not find them quite so useful. The fact is, I like to give the gentlemen of the press a wide berth. In this present case I don't imagine his lordship would like to see details advertised in the popular press. I have to serve the best interests of my client, even when I am not retained.'

'Why did you say you didn't want a fee for taking on this case?' I asked him.

'Oh, I don't know. I like to feel untrammelled. My methods, you see, are sometimes unsettling.' He gave a low chuckle. 'That is to say, they sometimes unsettle the client.'

'What do you think happened to Wilfred Rhodes early this morning?'

'I said, back at Baker Street, it was a "pretty puzzle", if you recall. It may not turn out to be so pretty, when you consider the situation poor Rhodes is in. There is still a large area of the unknown in this case, but we are off to a good start, having solved the *Italian* corner of the puzzle. Did he get into the cab of his own volition, or was he put into it? The puncture in his arm, what of that? Was it self-administered? What part did the red-haired cabbie play in this little drama? These are some of the questions we have to find answers to.'

'Should we go round to the boarding-house in Eversley Gardens, do you think? Looking for clues, I mean.'

Holmes rubbed his chin thoughtfully. 'The boarding-house—yes, we must not forget that as a line of enquiry. It might be useful to know something of the lie of the land round about Eversley Gardens. Our cabbie will have a street-map. Yes, it might be useful to study it for a while. I am glad to see you are beginning to agitate your grey matter. I believe this puzzle is beginning to engage your interest.'

I was certainly not thinking of the Oval at that particular moment. 'But what about the cryptic message,' I said, 'which I've got off by heart now—*sahib cricketer in good hands pray the Italian will keep alive.* Don't you think that you've solved it, except for the word *sahib*? Doesn't it point to the writer being an Indian. As for its cryptic form, surely that must be because it was composed in a hurry, and composed by somebody with a shaky grasp of the English language.'

'You may be right, my boy. You may be right,' said Holmes, dreamily gazing out of the cab window.

I saw that we had now arrived at King's

Cross Station. I thought it curious that I should spend the first two days of my sojourn in London making a tour of the great railway termini. Had I not had so much else to think of and wonder at, I might have been overwhelmed by my impressions of the metropolis, with its great thoroughfares, overflowing with traffic, and its tree-bordered squares and great buildings, some of them five storeys high.

The trap door lifted and the cabbie's face appeared. 'I'll park the cab at the end of the rank, guv. Stay inside and leave it to me. I'll have a search round for Ginger.'

A long line of waiting hansoms were parked alongside the kerb outside the station—a quick count and I made it sixteen. The cabbie walked the horse to the end of the rank and in a minute or two we had taken the seventeenth place. He jumped down and we saw him go off up the line; meanwhile, a clip-clop to the rearward announced the arrival of another hansom to join the rank.

Holmes sat, relaxed and patient. 'The

London cabbie is a resourceful and genial fellow,' he observed, 'and we've lighted on a prime example, I fancy. Some whimsical person described the hansom cab as "the gondola of the London streets".'

'Gondola—you mean, as in Venice? That's not bad. I believe *you* minted that expression, Mr Holmes, and are too modest to lay claim to it. I believe *you* are that whimsical person.'

'I assure you I am not,' said Holmes, calmly taking my lance upon his shield. 'Modesty is not one of my virtues—nor is whimsy my *métier*.'

A moment later we heard angry shouts from the rear. The 'gondola' immediately in front of us had moved up two places already, and it was clear that the 'gondolier' behind us considered us a stumbling-block to the desired rate of progress up the line. However, at last our man appeared, shuffling his feet in a clumsy attempt at running, and it occurred to me that he had spent so much of his life seated on his box that he had almost lost the use of his legs.

'I found Ginger, guv,' he panted. 'He's right up at the front of the rank. I asked him if he took a fare to the Italian 'ospital this morning and he said, yes, he did. Look, guv—it's time for me to swaller a cup o' Rosie. You get in Ginger's cab and he'll take you somewhere where you can 'ave a talk with him.'

Holmes acted swiftly and sprang out of the cab. He pressed payment into the cabbie's expectant palm and set off with a quick stride towards the front of the long line of waiting hansoms. I followed, half-running, at his heels. And, sure enough, there at the front stood a young cabbie with a heavily freckled face, holding the door of his cab back for us to step in. He wore a top hat, but a good deal of ginger hair was visible and covering the nape of his neck. Holmes paused only long enough to rap out: 'Take us to where you picked up the sick man early this morning.' Then we took our seats.

Passengers that had been disgorged from

a train a few minutes before were beginning to stream urgently across the forecourt, bent upon staking claims upon the front-rank hansoms. We were just in time.

'That was lucky,' I said.

'Luck plays its part,' said Holmes dryly.

So began another journey. I noticed at once that we were going back the way we had come, which was logical, because the place where Ginger Moxon had 'picked up the sick man'—the boarding-house—and the Italian Hospital—must all be in the same narrowly-confined area of London. I said as much to Holmes and he confirmed that this must be so.

'What is London but a patchwork of villages, Bloomsbury being one of them? It is noted for its hospitals, although its most distinguished building is the British Museum. When I first came to London I lodged in Montague Street, just round the corner from the museum.' He went on to reminisce about his early days in the capital, dubbing himself 'a Londoner by adoption'.

CHAPTER FIVE

We were clip-clopping along a quiet, tree-lined residential road when the horse was reined in and came to a halt. The trap-door lifted. 'This is it, guv—50, Swancombe Gardens.'

'Carry on for another hundred yards,' said Holmes, and the cabbie, accordingly, moved the cab forward. When we had halted again we climbed out and the cabbie jumped down. He then addressed a direct question to Holmes, a shade of anxiety in his tone 'Are you with the force, guv?'

Holmes disclaimed any connection with the police and assured Ginger that he was making enquiries in a strictly private capacity. He prompted him to tell the story of his taking the sick man to the Italian

Hospital in the early hours.

Ginger took a Woodbine from a packet, lit it and had a few puffs before he began. 'Well, it was this way. I kips in a street behind King's Cross Station. I'm on the mornings this week. There's always a few fares to be picked up at the crack o' dawn, like. People who want to catch the first trains to the North of England. I got to the yard at five—that's my starting time—and soon afterwards a telephone call comes through to the office and I'm sent off to 50, Swancombe Gardens, this house down the road here. It's a doctor, the clerk says—a foreign doctor by the sound of his voice—and its an emergency. I'm to take somebody to the hospital up the road. Well, I comes down this road and it was just about dawn time, but it was dark because the clouds were right low down. We'd 'ad a drop o' rain in the night but it wasn't raining.

'I pulled up outside No 50 and hops down off the box. A bloke comes staggering down the drive and through the open gateway and

I can see he's carrying somebody in his arms. It's a young feller he's carrying, wrapped up in a blanket, and he's unconscious by the look of him—eyes shut tight. Between the two of us we puts him in the cab, laying back on the cushions. "He ain't dead, is he?" I says, " 'cos I don't fancy carrying stiffs about." "No, no, no," he says, "but, quickly, get to the Italian Hospital as quickly as you can. That's the nearest hospital. You know where it is? It is not far." I says, "Yes, I know where it is—it's in Queen's Square." Then he hops in the cab.'

'Can you describe the man?' said Holmes.

Ginger took a few more puffs of his cigarette. 'Well, guv—allowing for the fact that I didn't see a lot of him, him being well wrapped up, and the weather being a bit nippy, I don't blame him—but he was an Indian all right. His face was as dark as Old Nick, and he spoke with a proper old Indian twang. I've run across a few while I've been cabbying. Anyway, I gets to the hospital, pulls up outside and a porter comes out. I jumps down and looks inside the cab and you could've knocked me over with a feather. There's only one of 'em inside—him as looks like a corpse. The Indian geezer's done a bunk. He musta took his chance just before we set off from outside his house—I remembered I'd had to go and pull the nag's head away from a bit o' grass verge he was nibbling at.

'Well, I thought to meself—there's something fishy about this. For all I know it's a corpse inside and I'm landed with it. So I said nothing to the porter except that the feller I'd brought was chronic sick and his case was urgent. Then I got away as quick as I could. I laid the whip on the nag. That's all I know about it, guv. I know 'ow you got on to me—me ginger 'air give me away, ain't that right? It's not a murder case, is it? You can lose a lot o' time and boodle appearing in court as a witness.'

Holmes reassured him on that point. He thanked him for his frankness and repeated that he had no connection with the law, that it was not a case of murder and that he was to feel quite easy in his mind. He asked him to wait until we had returned from an inspection of No 50, and borrowed his street-map.

That house, when we had strolled up to view it, proved to be a three-storey house with rain-washed ivy straggling over its dark red brickwork, set back about twenty-five yards from its gateway. A new-looking brass plate, fixed to the gatepost, read: *Pravad Nath Gupta—Physician & Apothecary.*

'Apothecary,' I whispered to Holmes, '—that's drugs, isn't it?' His eyes, however, were not on the brass plate but directed towards something at the roof-level of the house—I did not know what. It was clear he was intrigued by something he saw. 'Hmmm!' came from him, and then he signed to me that we were to stroll on farther down the road.

We halted at a corner. 'I should very much like to have a talk with Doctor Gupta. I believe we are standing at the edge of a web, and we have taken hold of a thread that may lead us to the centre of that web, where we may find a foul spider.'

A shiver ran down my spine. 'He doesn't put *Doctor* Gupta on his plate, or put any letters after his name.'

'I doubt if that has much significance,' said Holmes. 'It is not illegal to practise medicine without a qualification. It's a sore point with properly qualified men. I've heard my old friend, Watson, murmur against it. None of that bears much upon our problem—how to get inside and take the measure of Mr Gupta.'

'I know. You could pose as a government official and you've called to check the authenticity of his papers. You do have an air of authority. You could carry it off.'

'Indeed?' said Holmes. 'I hope I do not in the least resemble a government official. However, I am glad to see you are entering into the spirit of the thing. Of course, your idea won't do at all. The first thing he would do is to ask to check the authenticity of *my* papers, and where would that leave me? No, that won't do. Be comforted though. Many a man has started out upon a career as a private detective, brimming with confidence, and failed at it. He has then found his true niche as a writer of detective fiction, having a quantity of impractical notions in his head —and for the purposes of writing fiction the more impractical the better. No, I'll tell you how I propose to meet this difficulty.' He took a notebook from his inside pocket, tore out a page, produced a stub of pencil, wrote something on the page and handed it to me. 'Our mystery man,' he said, with a grim smile, 'is not the only one who can write eleven-word cryptic messages.'

The message read: *Imperative must see you. Your professional reputation in jeopardy. Sherlock Holmes.* I handed it back to him. 'I don't quite see.'

'There is nothing dearer to a professional man—nothing he is so sensitive about—as his reputation. And, I think, particularly in this case, where we are dealing with a man without the buttress of a qualification. I fancy that if we hand in this note he will read it and react swiftly, and we shall be ushered into his presence almost immediately.'

'Yes, but aren't you giving the whole show away. Won't it put him on his guard? Won't he recognise your name?'

'I hope he does recognise it. I will be honest with you—I am keeping back from you a vital piece of information I gleaned a little while ago. I will keep you in suspense. In the meantime, let us go and call on Mr Gupta. No, I think we had better call him *Doctor* Gupta in future.'

It was an Indian manservant who answered the door when Holmes had tugged the bell-rope. He said the doctor was not available until after half-past two. Holmes promptly played his card—the warning note—and it proved to be a trump. The servant took it away and, when he returned, he ushered us into a study-like room. Five minutes later Doctor Gupta entered. He was of middle height, strongly built, neatly and conservatively dressed.

Holmes accorded him a short bow. 'Doctor Gupta, I wonder if you have heard my name.'

'Yes. You are a detective. I cannot understand your note. Are you investigating a crime? What has it to do with me?'

Holmes, with an admirable economy of words, gave an account of 'a certain young man' who had been admitted to the Italian Hospital in the early hours of the morning; he went on to tell of Doctor Bartoli's diagnosis that he was suffering from the toxic effect of a drug overdose or misdose. He concluded: 'The cab-driver who brought him to the hospital has said to me, privately—that is to say, to me alone—that he received the sick man from the hands of an Indian doctor.'

Doctor Gupta, not surprisingly, looked startled at the last two words. His brow furrowed. 'I am the only Indian doctor in Bloomsbury.'

'Precisely, doctor—and that is why I have

called upon you. I feel that it is right and proper that you should be advised of what has happened, and warned of the potential threat to your reputation. I am being quite open with you because I am absolutely certain that you are not involved in this affair at all. You are entirely blameless.'

The doctor seemed a trifle taken aback. After a pause he said: 'I am certainly not involved in it. I know nothing of it. I began my work at half-past nine this morning—I did not rise until eight o'clock—and I have administered no drugs to anyone. I do, of course, keep a quantity of drugs here. I would like to know, however, why you are so certain that I am not involved.'

'Because,' said Holmes, 'you do not have a telephone installed in your house. I believe you did have one for a time.'

'You are quite right, Mr Holmes. I had one installed at the beginning of the year. I believed it would assist me in my practice, but I became more and more dissatisfied with it. I found it to be an intolerable intrusion and I had it taken away a week ago. I saw a good joke in *Punch* last week, in which a physics teacher says to his class: "What happens when a body is immersed in water?" and the bright student replies. "The telephone rings"—he is in the bath, you see.' He laughed.

Holmes did not smile, and I was surprised to see him lower his head and press his fingers hard upon his corrugated brow. After a while he lifted his head. 'Excuse me— Doctor Gupta, the person responsible for the serious condition of the patient in the Italian Hospital undoubtedly has a telephone installed in his house. He telephoned for a hansom to be sent to his house—'

'Then you know the address of the house?'

'Not at present. Doctor, I would like you to leave this matter entirely in my hands. Do not communicate with the police. I assure you that I have carried my investigation of the affair to the point where I am confident I can unravel the mystery in a few hours.'

'In a few hours! Mr Holmes, are you a

magician? I hope you will forgive me for saying that you do not look a well man—'

Holmes broke in abruptly: 'I will not take up any more of your time—I believe I have interrupted your rest period. Have I your permission to walk about the grounds of your house?'

'Oh, certainly.' He lifted his gaze to the ceiling for a few moments. 'I am trying to think of another Indian doctor—'

'No, no,' said Holmes, moving towards the door of the study, 'do not trouble yourself.'

'Ah, yes—you wish me to leave the matter in your hands. You are a man with a formidable reputation, and I am satisfied that you are acting in my best interests. Yes, by all means, examine the grounds.'

He escorted us to the front door. 'You will continue your investigation then. We have a proverb in India: *he who sits in the valley will not see the new moon set.*' He smiled and shook hands with us.

At the gate Holmes turned and directed

his gaze at the roof-level of the house. He glanced at me. 'Yes, the vital piece of information I gleaned when last I stood here and surveyed the house was that the telephone had been disconnected. You see, at the corner there, where the ivy has been pulled away—you can see four empty screw-holes in the brickwork. It suggested to me that Doctor Gupta was not implicated in the affair. It was a bold supposition but a correct one. The man we have just talked to would not have written *"sahib cricketer"*— the idea is preposterous.'

'But he must be implicated in the affair in some way,' I said. 'The cabbie said an Indian-looking chap staggered out from this gateway, carrying an unconscious man in his arms. The doctor looks hefty enough to be able to do that with ease.'

'He does indeed. I meant implicated in the sense of being guilty. I think what we are dealing with here is some kind of masquerade—some kind of cruel deception. However, to business. We have the doctor's permission to examine the grounds. Foot-prints are a speciality of mine. We may find some interesting specimens, for the ground is wonderfully soft after all the rain we've been having. Rain has its beneficial side—though it may spoil your senseless cricket matches.'

I now saw the Great Detective in his ele-ment, subjecting the driveway and the path which led up the side of the house to the rear to a close and patient scrutiny. He relied solely upon his keen eyesight, without bene-fit of his famous magnifying-glass. He walk-ed slowly, head bent down, across the lawn to the end section of the garden where there were a few stunted fruit trees and bushes.

He stopped suddenly and pointed to a footmark, well sunken into the soft earth. Its toe pointed towards the house. He placed his foot beside the mark and directed the full weight of his body downwards. 'You see the contrast,' he said. 'My print is shallow by comparison. I weigh twelve stone. A man carrying a dead weight of another man would be twenty stone at the very least.'

'The dead weight of another man being Wilfred Rhodes, is that what you think?'

'I am certain of it. The question we now have to find the answer to is—who did the carrying? It was not Doctor Gupta. I noticed that his feet were several sizes smaller than my own. These two prints we are looking at are the same length. He is not a man of middle height is our unknown masquerader. Let us look further.'

At the end of the garden was a small gate in the boundary fencing and it led into an alleyway which served not only Swancombe Gardens but also the next road. I noticed at once that the alleyway had many footprints in its mud, supplemented with wheelbarrow ruts, and I guessed it was for that reason Holmes did not attempt to pass through the gate. Instead he took the cabbie's street-map from his pocket and studied it. I, too, craned my neck at it.

'Here is Swancombe Gardens. We are facing north. The next road to the north would appear to be Monkleigh Gardens.' He stared hard at the backs of the houses before us. 'I think we will go round to Monkleigh Gardens—we may find something very interesting in that street.' He folded the street-map, returned it to his pocket and sighed: 'Lestrade—an old friend of mine in the constabulary, now retired—was a great believer in what he called "leg-work". I never have been, but it would seem to be unavoidable in this case.'

Thus we traipsed back down Doctor Gupta's garden and regained the road. Five minutes later we were strolling along Monkleigh Gardens, which did not differ greatly in character from Swancombe Gardens. Suddenly, Holmes clutched my arm. 'There!' he said softly. A few more paces brought us to a house with a somewhat tarnished brass plate on the gatepost. It read: *Dr Denzil Redthorn—M.D.* We exchanged glances.

'Is this "the enemy", Mr Holmes?' I asked him in a low, conspiratorial voice, as we stood staring at the lower front windows of the house.

'It may well be. You will not have failed to observe the telephone wires.' (I *had* failed to observe them—until he mentioned them.) 'Yes, I believe the enemy's position is now known to us. There remains the question of his defences, and I suggest we pay him a visit in order to test them.'

The thought flashed through my mind— but what about a stratagem?—and words, voicing that thought, were on the tip of my tongue. I kept silent and tamely followed him as he went towards the front door because I was struck with his appearance— he looked so tired and drained of energy. His carriage—usually so upright—had begun to droop at the shoulders.

Several tugs at the bell-pull failed to bring anyone to the door, although we faintly heard the bell clanging inside the house. Was the house unoccupied, I wondered, or was somebody lying low? After a few minutes we followed a path round to the back of the house and there, suddenly, we came

112

face to face with an elderly man, somewhat stooped, dressed in heavy boots, mud-stained corduroy trousers and coarsely-woven shirt, open at the neck. He held a spade in his hand.

'Good afternoon,' said Holmes. 'You are the gardener, I see. Is the doctor at home, can you tell me?'

'No zirr,' answered the old man. 'He gone off to the cricket Tass Match, zo he told me. You be a patient o' his'n, zirr?'

Holmes' eyes looked from left to right. 'No, not a patient. I wished to see him on a private matter. May I ask if you have been Doctor Redthorn's gardener for a long time?'

'Waal, I'm not his gardener, special-like. I gardens for three gent'men hereabouts.'

'Doctor Redthorn is a generous man, I believe.'

'Jann-rus!' The old man's tone of voice implied that it came as a shock to hear the doctor so described. 'I don't know what you call jann-rus. He's slow enough to stump up my four shillun at the end o' the week. He owes me more'n a pound.'

' Holmes said he did not like to hear of a workman being deprived of what was due to him and, somehow, by moving a step or two closer to the old man, a coin changed hands. I could not see if it were gold or silver but, whatever it was, it served to straighten the old fellow's back and predispose him to make any disclosures that might be called for. He glanced about him and then, with a beckoning nod of his silvery head, led the way round to the back of the house where, beside a potting-shed, stood an old but comfortable wicker chair. With a gesture he offered the seat to Holmes but Holmes indicated to the old man that he himself should take it. So indeed he did and, afterwards, took a clay pipe from his pocket and busied himself with cleaning it.

'You'm acquainted with Mizziz Redthorn, I rackon,' he said slyly. 'Or mebbe you'm a solicitor chap.'

'I am conducting an investigation on

114

behalf of somebody, it is true,' said Holmes. 'Not, however, Mrs Redthorn. I presume that lady is not living here now.'

The old man said that she had left the house two months before, taking with her a daughter aged eight years. Doctor Redthorn had come to Bloomsbury from Mitcham, in Surrey, in '96 or '97, he was not sure which. He was about thirty-five years old and, in his early twenties, had played regularly for Surrey County Cricket Club as an amateur. He had made his mark as a dynamic young batsman. Then his father had threatened to stop his allowance unless he gave up playing cricket altogether and got down to studying medicine. When he took up with the game again five years after he had made a poor showing. His skill and flair for batsmanship had deserted him. 'Seemed to be varry bitter about it. Still, he was a proper member of the club, like, and he knew 'em all up at the Oval—the Sec'et'ry chap, and all the others.'

'He knows Mr Alcock, the Club Secretary,

you say?' said Holmes.

'Aah, that's his name—Alcock. Aah, he knows him well enough. It were like he were a second father to him when he were making a big noise, before he took to studying to be a doctor. O' course, he bain't got a good word to say about Mr Alcock now, but then he bain't got a good word to say about anybody much.'

'And when did he take up drinking heavily?'

The old man looked surprised. 'You knows about that then?'

Holmes turned and pointed to a cardboard box, half-hidden behind the dustbin, from which the necks of half a dozen empty whisky bottles peeped out.

'You got sharp eyes, maister. Aah, he took up wi' drinking a year or two back. His business went on the slide, like—spashly after this Indian doctor started up nearby. Varry pop'lar man, from all accounts. You should hear Doctor Redthorn slanging him and calling him Gunga Din and I don't know what. He talks to me private, 'cos I don't think he got anybody else to talk to. I b'lieve he's got into trouble wi' owing people money, and he don't have enough patients to keep his head 'bove water.' He stared at Holmes, his eyes narrowing as he tried to puzzle out Holmes' interest in the matter. 'P'raps you come here about his owing money, eh?'

Holmes ignored the question. 'And his wife left him, taking the child, you say?'

'Aah, she went off a month or two back.'

'You saw him earlier this morning, I believe.'

'Aah, I come here soon after nine and he calls me into the house. "I'll just take my boots off," I says. "Never mind about that," he says. He's let the place go to rack and ruin, you know. He said he'd had an accident with his hand—he'd bandaged it and it'd come loose. He said he wanted a third hand, like, so I helped him bind it up and make a good job o' it. I saw these teeth marks across his fingers—real nasty-looking.'

'Where on the fingers?' said Holmes. 'Can you show me. I presume it was the left hand.'

'Aah, it were the left 'un,' replied the old man. He pointed to a place on the outside of his left hand, by the knuckle of his small finger. 'It were across these two fingers— the little 'un and the one next to it. He said a dog 'd snapped at him when he'd gone out for a walk early on. I said he'd better watch out because o' the rabies you hear tell of, but he said he were the doctor, not I. He were not in the best o' humour. Anyway, I helps him on with his coat and he says he's going off to the Oval to take his mind off his hand hurting him, but I seed him put a half-bottle in his pocket and I thinks to mesalf he favours that to take his mind off his hand, more 'n watching a blessed cricket match.'

'The house is locked, I suppose,' said Holmes.

'Aah, it will be,' replied the old man. 'Excuse me, maister, are you from the police?'

At this point of the interview Holmes brought into operation his evasive tactics—a curt expression of thanks and a bidding of good afternoon, the result of which was that we quitted the premises of Doctor Redthorn's house inside a minute. He had got the information he required and did not intend to dawdle, lest the effect of the coin that had changed hands began to wear off.

I could not with any accuracy say how long we had kept the cabbie waiting—it must have been close to an hour. He saw us approaching and was preparing to climb up on to the box when he noticed something I myself noticed at roughly the same time. Holmes had begun to falter as he walked, and his hand was clutching his chest. His face was ashen grey. The cabbie shuffled urgently towards us and, together, we supported the stricken man as his legs gave way.

'He don't look so clever, guv,' the cabbie said, looking at me. 'We'd better get him to a doctor. What about that doctor up the road?'

'No, no, no,' said Holmes, speaking with difficulty. 'Take me to Baker Street. No, no —not Baker Street. To Queen Anne Street. To Doctor Watson's house.'

'What number of the street, guv?'

'On the—left hand side. Look for—for a new brass plate. Help me—into the cab.'

We managed somehow to get him into the cab and he settled back with a huge sigh of relief. The cabbie mounted the box and away we started. At the motion Holmes groaned and gasped, but when we got fairly into our stride he closed his eyes and seemed to resign himself to the swaying and jolting.

My feelings can be imagined. I remembered that, before we left No 221b, I had questioned the wisdom of embarking on the investigation of the Rhodes mystery, bearing in mind his doctor's advice to take life more easily. There was no room in my mind now for any of the features of that mystery, and I gave no thought to the hapless Wilfred Rhodes, seriously ill, perhaps mortally ill, at the Italian Hospital: my sole concern now was for the condition of my tutelary genius, laid low, not by one of his adversaries—what chance had they to best him?—but by some cowardly physical disorder.

It seemed a long, long journey. Eventually we halted and the cabbie jumped down and put his head in. 'Is he all right, guv?' he said, by which, I believe, he meant to enquire if Holmes were still breathing. 'This must be the place. Name o' Watson. New brass plate, like he said. Let's get him out then. Gently does it.'

A few minutes later a maid opened the door of Doctor Watson's newly-established consulting-rooms and was confronted by three men, the tallest of them being supported by the other two. It was unlikely that she saw anything amiss in this, given the nature of her employer's business. It chanced that Doctor Watson had glimpsed us through the front, deeply-bayed window as we lurched up to the door, so that, before scarcely a word had been spoken, he appeared at the maid's elbow, almost brushing her aside in his agitation.

'My *dear* old friend—what, in heaven's name, has brought you to this pass? Bring him in. Bring him in.' He bid the maid fetch his bag to him. We brought the sick man into the middle of the hallway, where he was sufficiently alert to pay off the cabbie, who nodded briefly to me and retreated. Holmes then attempted to introduce me by mumbling: 'a young friend...Fairhurst...fine fellow.' The performance of this alliterative introduction taxed his strength and the doctor forbade him to talk further. He and I then assisted Holmes down the hall and into a small room that I took to be an emergency sick-room, it having a bed in it and not much furniture besides. There we helped him to remove his outer clothing as he sat weakly on the edge of the bed.

Doctor Watson went to the doorway and took his bag from the maid; he then asked me in a polite undertone to wait outside while he examined his old friend. Once out in the hallway I stood for a while at a loss. It occurred to me that there was nothing to prevent me walking out of the house if I so desired. The fact that I had no valise did not concern me much—I had some ready cash in a money-belt round my waist, and my letter of introduction to the man on the Board of Agriculture, to whose office in London, vast and alien as it was, I supposed I could find my way. It was, perhaps, not too late to do something in that direction that very day. No, there was nothing to prevent me going about my business exactly as I might have done had I not had a mishap in Marylebone Road.

And then Mr Holmes re-entered my thoughts and I knew that, of course, I could not leave the house without knowledge of his condition, be it better or worse. (This is, I trust, not an untimely moment to record that I had lost my father, my sole surviving parent, a few weeks after my twenty-first birthday, and I believe the fatherly interest Mr Holmes had shown in me had struck a responsive chord in me.)

After a while a lady with a matronly figure came through into the hall, smiled hospitably at me and said, with just a trace of embarrassment in her manner: 'You are...?'

'My name is John Fairhurst, ma'am,' I replied. At that moment the doctor emerged from the sick-room, put his finger to his lips and gently ushered us a few yards down the hall.

'How is he?' asked the lady quietly.

'My dear, you have not held luncheon, have you? You need not have waited. Have you met Mr Fairbanks?'

'Fairhurst,' I corrected him. It is strange how one is jealous of the correct form of one's name.

'Oh, forgive me—Fairhurst. He is a new friend of our patient. Perhaps he would like to partake of luncheon with us. You must persuade him to come and sit at the table with us.'

I was hungry and needed no persuasion. We moved into the dining-room and Mrs

Watson gave the word that we were to be served. I sat at the table and felt strongly that I was in the company of two very kind people, although I felt also that my connection with Sherlock Holmes had a great deal to do with their solicitude.

'Mrs Watson and I have a rule that I do not bring my medical practice to the dining-room table,' said the doctor. 'This is exceptional, however, and I think you would like to know that my old friend is in no real danger—his heart is a little tired, that's all. He needs a good, long rest.'

'Have you given him—'

'A sleeping-draught, my dear? Yes. He swallowed some and spilled the rest. He was never the most docile of patients. I think he will sleep for a few hours, when I hope to see him wake refreshed, and to see some colour return to his face. Now let us fall to and do justice to this cold beef. I understand you are a digger, Mr Fairhurst.'

Mrs Watson seemed midly shocked. 'John dear, that isn't a very polite expression. Our

125

guest will be offended.'

'No, not at all,' I said, trying to be amusing. 'A digger I am and a digger I'll be—until I shave off my beard and wear a fancy straw hat.'

'Do you mean to shave off your beard?' enquired the doctor.

'Well, I don't know yet if I *want* to merge with the natives—to fade into the background. I might prefer to stay a digger.'

'To remain an individual, you mean?' said Mrs Watson sympathetically.

'That word "digger"—I suppose it started in the Gold Rush days,' said the doctor. 'What would that be—forty or fifty years ago—about the time I was born. Is there any gold left in Australia? People still digging for it?'

I grinned. 'Well, you'll find a handful of optimists in every little community, all the world over.'

The doctor pointed his fork playfully at me. 'I hope that's not a reference to me starting up a new practice, young man.'

This was not half bad as a piece of wit, and I began to think that, in writing the Sherlock Holmes stories, he had represented himself as a bit of a dullard—when, in reality, he was not that at all. He asked me if my father had been born in the British Isles. I told him my grand-father, like Defoe's Robinson Crusoe, had been born and reared in the city of York, and had made the voyage to Australia in the most famous ship of that time. 'That was in the eighteen-fifties, and he made his way to the gold-fields of Ballarat. He made a fortune, but foolishly lost it by gambling and, consequently, my father was not born with a silver spoon in his mouth.'

'Shouldn't you have said "a gold spoon?" ' said the doctor, smiling. 'That ship that took him to Australia—the most famous ship of that time, did you say?'

'It was the s.s *Great Britain.*'

'Ah, yes—one of Brunel's ships, wasn't it?'

'It was the first iron ship, and the first

ship fitted with a screw propellor. She was an emigrant ship for a long time.'

'An emigrant ship, was she? I never knew that.'

'Yes, for many years. I believe she is now just a hulk at Port Stanley, in the Falkland Islands, and is used for storing coal in.'

'I say!' exclaimed Doctor Watson, looking sincerely aggrieved. 'That's a bit of a come-down, isn't it?'

After luncheon he took me into his study and the maid brought in coffee. I settled into an armchair. Before the doctor did likewise he peeped into the sick-room to satisfy himself that his patient was sleeping. 'Sleeping like a top,' he said when he returned. 'I should like to get him upstairs and into a comfortable bed. More than that, I should like to get him to stay here in this house for a few days. However, he is a law unto himself and may decide otherwise. I shall battle with him.' He took a pipe from a rack on the mantelpiece and sat down with a tobacco jar between his knees.

'I see you don't keep your tobacco in the toe of a slipper,' I said.

He laughed. 'Oh, you mean like Holmes. Yes, that is one of his little Bohemian ways. I should be interested to know how you came to be acquainted with him. Do you feel inclined to tell me the story?'

I willingly told him the story, and what I had to say was by way of being a synopsis of what I have written so far in this memoir. It occupied fully an hour in the telling. The doctor puffed at his pipe and interrupted me only three or four times to ask me to clarify a point.

'Well, I never!' he said, when I had brought the story to a dry-throated conclusion. 'Had I been involved in all this I should have called it "The Case of the Missing Cricketer." '

'Mr Holmes said you would have called it "The Case of the Missing No 11." '

'Did he, by Jove! "No 11" sounds rather too much like a London horse-bus, or one of these new-fangled trams. I say! It's to be hoped this cricketer chap will be none the worse for his experience. So he's in the Italian Hospital, is he? Do you know, I think I know that Doctor Bartoli—I met him somewhere—I can't remember where. The core of the mystery is—what precisely happened at this alcoholic doctor's place in the early morning? I'm fearful that when Holmes wakes up he will want to put his bloodhound's nose to the trail and try to pick up the scent again. I shall put a spoke in his wheel, if I can. I don't want to lose my old friend just yet. He talks about retirement, you know. Going in for bee-keeping down in Sussex. He was brought up near Hastings. Well, perhaps you don't know where Hastings is.'

'I've heard of the Battle of Hastings.'

The doctor laughed: 'Yes, and it will be a battle to keep him tethered here for a while, getting some much-needed rest. Well, young man, I suggest we go for a constitutional. Are you game?'

He had risen to his feet and I followed suit.

I was not quite clear what he meant. 'A constitutional—what's that?'

He laughed. 'Oh, you'll soon pick up the language. A constitutional is a walk—a stretching of the legs. We city-dwellers do it all the time.' We left the house. As we set off down the street he confided in me, saying that his proposal that Holmes should stay at his house might be countered by him expressing concern about his housekeeper. 'He is likely to raise that objection to the scheme—that she would worry about his not returning—unable to sleep—calling in the police—all that sort of thing. Actually, she would do no such thing, being quite used to his erratic ways, but that is the excuse he will make so that he may slip the leash. I know him of old. Well, I am going to leave a note at 221b, Baker Street. I don't think an interview with the dear lady will be necessary—in any event, she will be taking a siesta. You see my scheme then—when he raises his objections as aforesaid, I can testify—and you can lend your voice to it—

that Mrs Hudson has been informed, and assured that there is no cause for alarm.'

He executed his scheme as smoothly as he had outlined it to me, after which he led me off in the direction of Marble Arch for what he called 'a saunter in Hyde Park.' He showed me Tyburn Tree, the spot where the gallows had stood for more than six centuries. There was a triangular stone in the roadway that marked it.

'You know the expression, when we say somebody's "gone west"? Somebody's met his end? Well, that refers to this spot where we're standing now—where the gallows used to be. Tyburn was to the west of the City, d'you see?'

I shuddered to think of all the neck-stretching that had taken place in front of callous, jeering mobs—right where I stood. Doctor Watson seemed to be reflecting along the same lines, for he continued: 'Not many comical things have happened here, I imagine. There is one on record though. It concerns five rogues who were due to be strung up and had been stripped of their clothes accordingly. The clothes of a gallows-bird became the property of the hangman, you see. Well, a reprieve came for the five men. The hangman would not let go of his "perks" and so the quintet had to walk back to the City in the altogether. Funny sight, I dare say, what?'

'In the altogether—what does that mean?' I said.

'Oh, you haven't caught up with the modern slang. Good for you! It means, not having a stitch on. Naked as the day they were born.'

We ventured into the park a little way and stood with a good-humoured crowd of park strollers, listening to a military band in brilliant scarlet uniforms who played stirring martial music. This was very much to the taste of Doctor Watson, and to me also.

When we at last re-traced our steps to Queen Anne Street and got back into the house we found that the doctor's scheme was already starting to go awry. Sherlock Holmes was not in bed in the sick-room—he was in the dining-room and, as we entered, he was wiping his mouth with his napkin, having just finished a plate of cold beef.

'Watson, so here you are—and my trusty Antipodean friend, whom I was sure would not abandon me—have you been out walking? Capital! The exercise will do you good. I thought you were looking a bit puffy around the gills.'

Mrs Watson, at that moment, came into the room with a pot of coffee in her hand. She looked a trifle shamefaced. 'John, dear, Mr Holmes insisted on getting up, dressing, washing—well, he said he was famished.' She poured a cup of coffee for her guest, who seized it and gulped it down thirstily.

'Look here, Holmes,' said the doctor in aggrieved tones—'this is just like you. If you have any ideas about rushing off on this cricketer business I suggest you dismiss them from your mind.'

'My dear Watson, you are at liberty to suggest it, but I am not bound to act upon your suggestion.'

'I say, this is pretty high-handed of you. I do feel you owe me something.'

'Owe you something. No question about it. I owe you more than any other man living. But haven't I repaid some of it? I sang your praises to your good lady when you were courting her—isn't that so, Mrs Watson?'

'Never mind all that nonsense. Will you return to bed and favour your racked nerves with the benefit of a good, long rest. You know your heart is under strain.'

'Oh, come, Watson, you make too much of it. A couple of hours sleep has revitalised me, and my nerves are perfectly all right. I am grateful to you, of course. You were my port in a storm. And I am equally grateful to young Fairhurst here, who has been a splendid *aide-de-camp*—quite in the Watson tradition. I do not deserve to be supported by such staunch friends. However, I cannot stay here—you know Mrs Hudson frets and worries when I do not appear.'

'You know perfectly well she does no such thing. In any case, I have left a note for her.'

'Of course you have. I did not suppose you had gone off to stroll about aimlessly, particularly since, as I learned from Mrs Watson, you took your daily constitutional just before I arrived on your doorstep.'

'Holmes, you are the most exasperating friend a man ever had, I do declare—' This exchange was interrupted by the maid who entered and informed the doctor that a lady had called and wished to consult him.

'Ha! A patient for you, Watson,' said Holmes, 'and, I imagine, a fat fee. Fairhurst, we can now retreat under cover of this diversion.'

Doctor Watson glared at him for a few fraught seconds, then turned and quitted the room. Five minutes later Holmes and I were sitting back in yet another cab; it was the third we had hired that day and Holmes had leapt into it in such a manner as to confirm that he had entirely thrown off the disorder that had enfeebled him. The instruction he had given the cabbie— 'To the Kennington Oval, and lose no time!'—might have thrilled me had I not glimpsed a newspaper-seller's placard just as I was about to step into the cab. It read: 'England collapse. 48-5 at lunch.'

My feelings were mixed. I was pleased and proud that Australia had demonstrated her superiority over the Mother Country yet again, and had now, surely, won the series— not narrowly, but by three matches to none, with two drawn. At the same time, the likelihood that we should arrive at the Oval in time to see any play was as remote as that the sun would turn a cart-wheel in the sky. Of course, I had no knowledge of what Holmes intended to do when we got there. I enquired about this.

'Dear old Watson,' he murmured, turning aside my question. 'It's just as he says, I do exasperate him. I must make my peace with him when next I see him.' He turned to me. 'Intend to do? Why, we must see if we cannot run to earth this Doctor Denzil

Redthorn. We must strike while the iron is hot. Alcock, the Club Secretary, knows him, and that will assist us greatly. He will be sitting in the Members' Stand. Will he be nursing his remorse for whatever dreadful deeds he has committed? More likely he will be feeding his schoolboy illusions, as do all spectators of games of pat-ball. I presume the Members' Stand enjoys a degree of exclusivity. We shall be able to keep him under surveillance, and when the match is over—'

I burst in with: 'But, Mr Holmes, the match is *already over*!'

This drew from the Great Detective the sharpest look I had yet been subjected to. I felt a tremor of fear. 'What do you mean?' he said. 'Are you clairvoyant?'

'No, I am not clairvoyant—I have taken a leaf out of your book and used my powers of observation. That ought to please you. Just as I was about to step into the cab I saw a newspaper-seller's placard. England have collapsed. The lunch-time score was 48 for 5. They have lost half their wickets, and all their best batsmen are back in the pavilion—48 for 5 was the score an hour and a half ago. It must be all over by now.'

Holmes stared at me without speaking for a while. Then he said: 'Everything has gone so smoothly so far. I saw it as a miracle when my weakness fled from me an hour ago, as I lay on that sick-bed. You know how I hate stagnation of any kind. I felt as though I had awaked from the dead. This is disconcerting news you give me. Perhaps you had better explain, in simple terms, precisely what has been happening in this contest. In ordinary circumstances, it would be information of a kind I should not seek, but would prefer to leave unread in the sporting pages of the newspapers I take. However, circumstances alter cases.'

I spelled out the story of the match in statistical outline. Australia had batted first and had accumulated 324 runs. (My mind flew back to White Beard, the old gentleman on the train from Southampton to Waterloo, who had nettled me by saying: 'Damn Australians batted and made 324, all out.') England had responded with 183. The Australians had batted for the second time and made about 120. (This was a guess, as I had no way of knowing how many runs the last two batsmen had added to the overnight total.) Therefore England had started their second innings—the last innings of the match, in which the outcome of the match was to be decided—in search of something in the order of 260 runs to win.

'And that, sir, is a pretty formidable packet of runs to make on the last day of a Test Match, with the wicket possibly difficult after rain, and certainly worn. Wickets do wear, you know, just like the soles of the shoes you walk about in—and it makes batting more difficult. We know that they lost half their wickets for a miserable 48 runs at lunch-time. And, remember, there is no No 11 available to bat. He is *hors de combat*, as we know only too well. You see how hopeless England's position was when they restarted after the lunch interval. The match must be over by now.'

'My boy,' said Holmes, in his most saga-
cious of tones, 'you have told the story of
the match with admirable clarity, but you
have anticipated the outcome. Now you cannot deny that. And it is always dangerous
to anticipate. Morever, you have omitted
three important considerations.'

'What, only three!' I put in, sarcastically.

'No, you may have ten, if you wish.'

'Surely, Mr Holmes, you are not presum-
ing to know more of the state of the match
than I do.' I thought to myself—'Beware,
Sherlock Holmes—you may be walking into
a minefield.'

'In your summing-up,' said Holmes calmly. 'I heard no mention of the Spanish
Armada. No mention of Agincourt. No
mention of Trafalgar.'

'Trafalgar! What has that got to do with
it?'

'It has everything to do with it. You are
not allowing for the indomitable spirit of
the English. You should understand. You

are English by derivation, aren't you?'

Now I was really nettled. 'Hold on! Are you trying to make out I'm an Englishman? *That* I'm not! I'm an Aussie first and last. Australia, in case you don't know it, is fifteen thousand miles from England. I ought to know. I've done it by ship, and for the first time since I arrived here I wish I hadn't.'

'My dear Fairhurst—there's no need to get hot under the collar.' The tone of Holmes' voice sounded genuinely pained.

'I'm sorry.' I slumped back in my seat and breathed hard. Luckily, I cool down very quickly. 'Anyway, Mr Holmes, give me leave to predict that when we get to the Oval we will meet thousands of disappointed spectators streaming away from the ground. The ground will be empty and the match over. And, before we leave the subject, Australians are not lacking when it comes to indomitable spirit either.' And, to myself, I added: 'Put that in the toe of your slipper and smoke it!'

Holmes contented himself with saying: 'Well, I dare say you are right.' He did not seem at all put out.

Twenty minutes elapsed and Holmes was silent until we crossed the wide sweep of the Thames. 'Vauxhall Bridge,' he muttered. We rattled down some streets a good deal less elegant than those we had passed along on the north bank of the river. Soon the trap door lifted and the cabbie called out: 'Oval Cricket Ground, guv. What part? Turnstiles?'

'No, the main entrance,' replied Holmes, bent forward eagerly. I then saw the high outer walls of the great cricket ground (in those days, not a whit less famous than Lord's) and, to my surprise, saw that far from there being disappointed spectators streaming away from the ground, as I had predicted, people were streaming *towards* it. It was the backs of people I saw, not the faces. This was an astonishing turnabout of my preconceived ideas. A feeling of excitement gripped me. I knew then that the match was still in progress and that a dramatic finish was being fought out behind the high walls.

We stopped in the driveway of the main entrance and I stole a glance at Holmes. My arrogant prediction that the match would be over when we arrived had been wrecked and he was now presented with a superb opportunity to wither me with a cutting remark. He said nothing and we climbed out of the cab.

At that moment a great, thunderous roar was heard from inside the ground. It made me quiver and tingle to hear it. The roar continued for a full minute and it was made up, I imagined, of combined shouting, cheering and hand-clapping. Even Sherlock Holmes, the mocker, seemed to be stunned by it. He paused, lifted his head and seemed to sniff the air as if he had caught a whiff of cordite, following a great explosion. I longed to be there on the other side of the walls, to see what was happening. The home team were fighting their way out of trouble, that was clear; but the Aussies were fighters too. Would the English, inspired by the emotion of the crowd, break loose from the Aussie stranglehold?

My wits were in a whirl as I followed in the wake of Sherlock Holmes as he strode to the gate-house and spoke to two uniformed men at the open window. The noise had subsided but, even so, I had difficulty hearing what he said, although he spoke loudly and authoritatively. '...greatest urgency...Mr Alcock immediately...a matter of life and death...' I caught these shreds of his speech. I saw that he had switched on the full power of his personality—the dark, satanic side, with chin out-thrust and eyes blazing. A side door was opened, we went in and, with scarce a second's delay, were escorted down a corridor, up a full flight of stairs—another corridor and more stairs—and then through a throng of Members, blocking the way, their backs to us, on tip-toe, fidgeting and straining to see the cricket action.

Our escort forced a way through and we followed, and so we came up into the bright daylight of the arena. Before us lay green grass and white-flannelled figures.

At that precise moment we were halted, at the crest of the steps, by the most dramatic and chilling sound I had ever heard in my life. 'AAAaaaah!' It was an arpeggio of descending notes, expressive of the most heart-rending grief and sorrow, such as might have issued from the throats of any who witnessed the Massacre of the Innocents. I focused my gaze and saw that a catch had been made at deep square leg. The Aussie fielder had tossed the ball high in the air (it came to earth he knew not where) and half a dozen of his team-mates were moving in swiftly to clap him on the back and shake his hand, working it like a pump-handle.

What had happened? Who was out? I searched for the scoreboard and, shading my eyes, saw that the score was changing to 187 for 7 wickets, and the batsman who had been caught had made 104. That thunderous roar, when Holmes and I had stood by the gate-house, must have signalled his reaching a century.

Then I became aware of clapping erupting all around me, and growing by degrees ever louder and more vehement. All those seated in the Members' Stand now rose to their feet. It was the same all around the ground, and so began a cheering and shouting which combined to make a truly frightening noise.

I saw that the batsman who had lost his wicket was approaching the pavilion steps. He was coming straight towards me. He was not tall, but was stockily built, with a face that was broad and pugnacious. It flashed through my mind that this must be the great English hitter, Gilbert Jessop.

CHAPTER SIX

To set his foot on the steps and make progress he had to push past blazered Members who stood unhelpfully in his path, trying to clap him on the back. *He brushed past me.* Never again, I thought, would I be so close to the pulsating heart of a great sporting drama. (I was wrong, as will appear.)

Another white-flannelled figure brushed past me from behind—a taller man than Jessop. It was the next batsman in the batting order, on his way to the middle. I realised that where I was standing I was something of an obstruction. Where was Mr Holmes? I looked about me and saw that he was seated beside two men, recognizable as Lord Hawke and Mr Alcock. There was no vacant seat on that side, however.

I looked away to my left and, to my surprise, found that a familiar face was turned in my direction. It was no other than White Beard, as large as life. Oh, yes, he would be cock-a-hoop at England's fight back. He was beckoning to me and indicating a vacant seat beside him so, with some hesitation and some misgivings, I moved down the steps and edged along to the proffered seat.

'My boy, have you only just arrived?' he asked, his pale blue eyes shining. 'Did you see Jessop's innings?'

I shook my head.

'What, you didn't see it? Oh, I pity you. You have missed the experience of a lifetime. The most splendid exhibition of scientific hitting I have ever seen, and I've been watching cricket at the highest level for more than forty years. I never saw such an astonishing display of fireworks. Jessop's the man of the hour, I can tell you. Simply tore himself loose like a catapult. It was something to wonder at. Scoreboard couldn't keep up. Twice he hit the ball into the gallery—up there, above us. The second time a great cheer went up—I think some Johnny caught it. You know what W.G said when he first saw Jessop bat? "Well," he said—"we've found something this time." He spoke the truth. I tell you, I'm half-cracked with delight. Trust an Englishman to fight back from the edge of disaster, what! And in Coronation Year too. Don't you feel proud, my boy?'

I stiffened. 'I hope you've not forgotten that I'm an Australian, sir.'

'Eh? Oh, of course. Damn fine fellows, Australians. Always said so. Damn near as British as we are. Always give us a hard fight.'

It was on the tip of my tongue to say: 'Yes, and usually give you a beating!' I was irritated because, wonderful knock or no wonderful knock, it had been Jessop who had run out my hero, Victor Trumper, in our second innings. I turned my gaze towards the middle. 'Who's the new batsman, sir?'

'Johnny Lockwood,' said White Beard. 'Here, take my score-card.'

On the score-card I saw that he had pencilled: "263 to win." He had clearly written that at the start of England's innings. I glanced at the scoreboard. 187 for 7 wickets. That meant that England had to score another 76 runs to win the match, and after Lockwood there was only Lilley, the wicket-keeper, to go in. Assuredly, there would be no No 11. The situation for the home team was not rosy—76 runs being a tall order at the best of times. It was less rosy than White Beard and the crowd knew.

Suddenly a thought struck me that sitting, perhaps close to me in the Members' Stand, was somebody who also knew that No 11 would not walk out to bat, and that somebody was Doctor Denzil Redthorn. Was the worry gnawing at his conscience, as the moment, approached when No 11 might be called upon to go to the wicket, that Wilfred Rhodes' non-appearance would be entirely owing to some misdeed of his that he had cunningly schemed to cover up. But that was all banished from my thoughts as Hugh Trumble ran up to bowl to Lockwood.

In the next ten minutes Lockwood effectively played a dead bat to the few balls he received, while Hirst pushed the score along with ones and twos.

'See how cleverly Hirst is shielding Johnny Lockwood,' said White Beard. 'He's a past-master at that sort of thing. He does a lot of that when he's teamed up with the rabbits —for Yorkshire, in the county games.'

'Rabbits!' I queried. 'What rabbits?'

'The fellows who can't bat for toffee. The tailenders.'

It was when the 200 was being applauded that I glanced across to my right and saw that Holmes, Lord Hawke and Mr Alcock had got up and were edging towards the aisle. Looking directly at me—I was about twenty feet away—Holmes raised a finger, a sign I translated as 'Wait there!' It suited me down to the ground for I was completely gripped by the contest in the middle. It seemed to me that Lockwood was sometimes playing back when he should have been playing forward, and I felt sure he was going to be trapped lbw at any moment. Then the fat would be in the fire for England.

A further twenty minutes ensued of perilous survival from Lockwood, while Hirst was grafting for ones and twos. Then Trumble decided to bowl round the wicket to Lockwood. I felt in my bones that he would now trap the Englishman. At that moment I became aware that Holmes was standing in the aisle and, when he was satisfied that I had seen him, he inclined his head towards the top of the steps. The gesture was unmistakeable. He wanted me to vacate my seat and join him on the steps. To turn my back on the cricket action, and to involve myself anew in the case of the missing No 11.

I had come fifteen thousand miles to savour the sweetness of sitting and watching these two national sides locked in a struggle for supremacy. For a few moments rebellious feelings welled up inside me.

'Who's that Johnny?' I heard White Beard mutter. 'Looks like a foreigner. D'you know him?'

I turned to him and forced a smile. He was a fearful old chauvinist—but then, if it came to that, I was a fearful young one. 'He's a friend. I must go.'

He looked shocked and incredulous. 'What, go? Good God, you'll not see the end of the match!'

I had decided it would be the behaviour of a sulking child if I shook my head and remained seated. The good opinion of me that I hoped he had formed would be irretrievably lost. Besides—and this was a slightly absurd consideration—I was not a member of Surrey County Cricket Club and had not paid for my seat.

When I got to where Holmes stood he said nothing. He led the way up the steps, but no sooner had we passed into the shadowy recesses of the pavilion than a loud, prolonged groan reached our ears, and the anguish in it recalled the great 'AAAaaaah!'

that had signalled the dismissal of Gilbert Jessop. I heard someone close by shout: 'Lockwood's out! Leg before!' So, I thought, Trumble trapped him at last. I had guessed he would.

We carried on down corridors, moving away from the throng of Members, and entered a large room.

I was startled to find three men standing by a large office desk, all facing towards Holmes and me. There was an uncanny silence. We all stood there as if posing for a tableau. The three men were Lord Hawke, Mr Alcock and another man, just above medium height, with a weather-tanned face, and wearing a monogrammed blazer over white flannels. It dawned on me that they were staring at *me*. I gulped.

Lord Hawke broke the silence. 'Yes,' he said, and his eyes bored into me. 'Yes.' He said it again, and then, turning to the white-flannelled man I had not so far identified, he said: 'Maclaren—I brought you into this because I felt it only right you should know

155

what we are proposing to attempt. However, since we have not consulted you as to the ethics of the matter, you will not be required to admit that you know anything of it—I mean that, should it all go wrong, that you had any prior knowledge of it. You had better cut off to the pavilion. Whatever you say there—and, of course, you will be as tight-lipped as possible—there will be no perjury in it. I am the source of all the information you have. If it is false information, the blame attaches to me. Of course, there may not be time to set the ball rolling. You understand?'

Maclaren—and I knew that to be the name of the England captain—glowered at me for a moment, shrugged his shoulders and went out. I gulped again.

Lord Hawke turned to the Club Secretary. 'Mr Alcock, the accoutrements, without delay. Mr Holmes will attend to the other matter. Time is short.'

Mr Alcock left the room directly. A few seconds later Maclaren's head was thrust in at the door. 'Lockwood's out. Damn!

Lilley's at the crease. Better call it off.'

'No, no, Mclaren,' said Lord Hawke forcefully. 'Carry on!' Maclaren gave another shrug and shut the door.

Throughout all this talk, and comings and goings, I was as bewildered as ever I had been in my entire life. I could not tumble to what was going on. I could not imagine *if* it concerned me, and *if* it concerned me, *how* it concerned me. I knew absolutely nothing, but I intuitively guessed that Holmes, for all that he had not uttered a word since I had entered, had lit a fire under a cauldron and was stirring it vigorously. Clearly, he had done a great deal of talking in my absence.

'Holmes,' said Lord Hawke, very solemn-faced, 'I am taking on trust what you have told me. As a man of business I have made investments in my time—some good, some bad. If we go forward in this stratagem, as you call it, I shall be investing very heavily in your reputation. However, the die is cast. I have decided to back you and when I back somebody I back them to the uttermost. That is my character. I am a resolute person. You will search in vain, north or south of the river Trent, for anyone willing or able to challenge that statement. Now I must leave you—I must keep in touch with what is happening on the field. I hope you understand that we may have thirty minutes, but, equally, we may have only three, and that may be too few. That is the position. Carry on!'

He went out. Holmes swiftly set two chairs in the centre of the room and bade me sit on one of them. He reversed the other and sat astride it. We were face to face. He rested his arms on the chair-back and leaned forward, that familiar blaze in his eyes.

'My boy, I have told his lordship and the Secretary just as much as I think they should know, for my purposes. You follow me? For my purposes. What I have done is this—I have devised a stratagem within a stratagem, because I not only want Redthorn's villainy exposed—I want everyone to hear the truth from his own lips. We cannot be certain of learning the truth by any other means. By the way, he is sitting four or five places to the left of the seat you occupied, and one or two rows down. He was pointed out to me by the Secretary. What I did not tell the Secretary and Lord Hawke was that I knew to which hospital Rhodes had been taken. Do you see? There are half a dozen hospitals in that area. I convinced them that it would take days to locate him and, in the meantime, the doctors treating him might be in the dark as to the cause of his malaise and, of course, that part of my story accords with fact. Who but Redthorn knows? I said he might be close to death—I frightened them with that. I have persuaded them that, by adopting my stratagem, Redthorn can be exposed *within an hour*, and the truth uncovered and action taken—perhaps with the effect of saving his life at the eleventh hour.'

I was totally at a loss. 'Mr Holmes, I don't understand what all this has to do with me!'

The Great Detective took a firmer grip on

the chair-back. 'My boy, do you remember when we met Doctor Bartoli at the Italian Hospital? I passed you off as Rhodes' brother, remember? The idea came to me because I had noticed the resemblance you bore to the photograph of Rhodes that his lordship left with me at Baker Street. Do you remember Doctor Bartoli staring hard at you and saying: "Yes, I can see the family like-ness?" You do indeed uncannily resemble Rhodes, except that your face is bearded. With your chin shaven and your moustache trimmed more to the English fashion, I wager Rhodes' own mother could not tell you apart. You are the same height and weight—give or take an inch—give or take a pound. You are a cricketer. I am asking you to masquerade as Rhodes, if and when occasion serves. You will understand the state of the match better than I do, but it seems likely that No 11 will be called upon to bat. You heard what Lord Hawke said: "It may be thirty minutes, or it may be three." It will take me two minutes to shave your chin. Behind you is the Club Secretary's wash-room, with scissors, razor, soap and hot water. The Secretary is bringing Rhodes' cricket-bag, which George Hirst brought with him from the boarding-house. He is having to employ caution because, I freely admit it, this is a conspiracy—only five or six people are to know anything about it. So—you will go out to bat. The crowd will be deceived. Among the crowd is Redthorn, and he will be deceived. The moment the match is over—and who can predict what the result will be?—the Secretary will approach Redthorn and ask him to step into his office. The drama will be played out here. Lord Hawke and I will be here. Redthorn will think we know everything, having got it from Rhodes. We can wring the truth from him—the full facts as to what happened in the early hours of this morning. In the last resort—if he persists in vehemently denying everything—*you*, when you have returned from the field of play, can confront him, pointing the accusing finger at him, saying

"That's him!" He must crack then. Will you do it?"

Holmes' hypnotic eyes were boring into mine, but there had been nothing of pleading in that 'Will you do it?' It had been a straight question, calling for a straight answer. Alas, I found I could not give a straight answer, although I love straight answers as much as life itself. I had to raise an objection which seemed to me, at the time, quite overwhelming.

'I am an Australian, sir. I can't play for England!'

Holmes' lips went thin and white with annoyance, and his back stiffened. 'Play for England! I'm not asking you to play for England. I'm asking you to help me to lay a villain by the heels—to expose him and prevent a terrible injustice being done to an innocent man.'

I felt very confused. I felt I had lost the thread—.

'What innocent man? I'm not sure I understand. What has Doctor Redthorn—?'

'You've not forgotten Doctor Gupta, I trust. Don't you see that, as matters stand now, a police investigation would lead straight to him. On circumstantial evidence, as Redthorn has fabricated it, he would seem to be the guilty party. My boy, cricket is only a pastime. It's the same game of pat-ball the peasants played on the village green in the days of the Plantagenet kings. In those days it was a relaxation after a day's labour in the fields. Today, when we have professional cricketers, it has become the very day's labour itself. It is all out of proportion. Is the pursuit of a leather ball to take precedence over the pursuit of justice? There can be but one answer. Come—to the washroom!'

Willy-nilly I was jockeyed into the adjacent wash-room and Holmes was scissoring my beard before I had time to make further protest. It had taken me six months to grow but it was scissored and shaved off in under five minutes.

'Would you—ow!—describe yourself as a

163

tonsorial artist?' I enquired of Holmes.

'Don't talk!' Holmes replied. He added: 'One of my forebears was an artist.'

'A tonsorial artist?'

'Don't talk! No, no, no. A painter. I believe I have something of the artist in me.'

After having, rather impudently, said: 'No harm in believing,' I obeyed his command to keep silent while he shaved my neck and chin with a fearsome-looking cut-throat razor. At last he turned to wipe the razor.

'I read somewhere,' I said, 'that we have four selves. My self as I really am. My self as I think I am. My self as others see me— and my self as I think they see me. Four selves, and all likely to be different. What do you think?'

'Your self as I see you now is—'— he paused, took up the photograph he had in his pocket and studied it—'—a remarkable likeness to Wilfred Rhodes and, at the moment, putting aside your philosophizing, that is all I am concerned with.'

After I had rinsed and dried my face I

heard the door of the office open and the sound of something weighty being dumped on the floor. It proved to be Mr Alcock with Rhodes' cricket-bag—so large and capacious I would have thought it needed Sandow, the strong man, to lift it. Mr Alcock, who was, I judged, past sixty, was breathing hard.

'Good Lord!' he exclaimed when he looked up and saw my changed appearance. 'No question, Mr Holmes—he resembles Wilfred all right. Do you know, I do believe the eyes are the same colour. I had my doubts, but—'

'I've removed the beard, and your doubts, eh?' said Holmes, with a soft chuckle.

Well, I had come from the barber's and now I went to the outfitter's. The white flannel trousers fitted me well enough, and likewise the shirt and the sweater. Pads were buckled on my legs. They seemed very heavy and I commented on it.

'You'll need all the protection you can get,' said Mr Alcock grimly. 'Saunders doesn't bowl donkey drops.' He must have detected a shudder running through me after hearing those cheerless words because he stood up, took a small flask from his hip pocket and pressed it to my lips. He overcame my reluctance by tipping the flask so that I had either to take some into my mouth or suffer it to spill down my shirt.

He put away the flask. 'Mr Holmes, I trust you understand that with George Hirst and Arthur Lilley batting like Trojans your stratagem may never be put into operation. There may be no opportunity.'

'Yes, yes—I quite see that,' said Holmes testily.

'And one more thing. Were it not that the M.C.C Secretary, who is the real power on the Board of Control, had to stay at home with the onset of his sciatica, this stratagem would have been a non-starter. He would never have stood for it. Lord Hawke's position, as he has said, is that having started down a road he never turns back. For myself, my reasons are personal. Denzil Redthorn is well-known to me. I took him under my wing when he was a boy of eighteen and helped him all I could. He had two fine seasons for Surrey. However, I thought it right to lend my voice to his father's when his father urged him to give up cricket —which he considered had become an unhealthy obsession with him—and do his five years of medical study. In due course he qualified as a doctor and then he came back here to play for the county. He made a series of low scores and the day came when he had to be dropped from the side. It wasn't that he was rusty. He had got in with a wild set of medical students, so I heard, and had neglected his physical condition. I supported him as best I could but, in one of the most unpleasant scenes in my entire life, he rounded on me and accused me of betraying him. He said I had wrecked his chances of an England cap.

'I saw him then for what he was—a mean-spirited young scoundrel. I tell you, I should dearly love to hear him sing small. That, in a nutshell, is why I am backing you in this affair.'

'I see,' said Holmes laconically. 'Now I must see his lordship.'

'Yes, and I must show myself. I'll go with you.' Mr Alcock turned to me and told me to stay in the office and await the summons —if the summons were to come. He placed a hand on my shoulder and gripped it reassuringly.

They went out and I was left alone.

I took up Rhodes' bat. It was a Crawford's—a popular make—and it looked as if it had been well looked after, despite having seen a great deal of use. I was glad it was not a fearfully heavy bat, such as the blacksmiths and stonemasons back home used to wield.

As I made a few airy practice shots with it I recalled the knobstick I had fooled about with in Holmes' sitting-room at Baker Street, indulging a whimsical fancy that I was Australia's No 11, arriving at the crease with only four runs needed for a famous victory in a Test Match against England. I recalled my arrogant driving of the first ball to the boundary. Fantasy now trembled on the brink of being translated into reality. The trouble was that, in the process, something had got terribly distorted.

It could, surely, not be right that I should score the winning run for England.

Ten minutes later, with great suddenness, the door burst open. Lord Hawke entered, followed by Sherlock Holmes.

'Lilley's out. Played like a hero. Fifteen runs to win. Are you ready?' He stared at my changed appearance. 'By George, you could be his twin brother. By the way, are you a right-hander?'

I nodded, and opened my mouth to say that I was also an Australian, but I was not quick enough.

'Thank the Lord for that! Rhodes bowls with his left and bats with his right. Listen, young man! I've managed to get a message to George Hirst. The message was: "Lord Hawke says Play On." Now if he says any-thing to you when you get out there, just repeat the message. Don't linger. Hirst is a great talker, given half a chance. Get straight to the crease and take guard. Middle and leg. Put your gloves on as you walk to the wicket. Where's your cap? Put your cap on. Right! Come along!'

And so I went along. I went out to bat for England.

With bat and batting gloves in hand, I, the puppet, followed the two puppet-masters down the corridor and round and about until we had to force a way through the throng of high-spirited Members at the top of the stairs. It was a rowdy reception, with salutations and shouts of encouragement bombarding my ears from all sides, and it was startling to hear 'Good old Rhodes!' chorused at me. The masquerade had met its first challenge and was holding up well.

Suddenly I noticed that I was alone, the puppet-masters having halted. I had felt a pat on the shoulder and that was all. Trembling in the legs I went down the few remaining steps and stepped on to the green turf

of the Kennington Oval. It was close-crop-
ped and yielded excitingly to my tread. The
atmosphere crackled with high-tension elec-
tricity, and the hubbub was frightening.
Twenty thousand pairs of eyes were fixed
upon me and it made me feel distinctly
uneasy. The applause was for the real
Wilfred Rhodes who, although he had not
been among the wickets in this, the Fifth
Test, had performed very creditably in the
other four Tests. In the First Test he and
George Hirst had shot out Australia for 36
runs on a rain-affected pitch.

When I had my gloves firmly fitted on I
tried to get my bearings. I saw that all but
one or two of the fielding side were looking
straight at me as I approached. It made me
drop my head, but I jerked it back up de-
fiantly. I tried to locate Saunders and Trumble, who were to bowl to me. I had seen
them at Melbourne the year before and could
recognize them well enough. I saw Trumble,
who was nearly a foot taller than me, standing beside one of the umpires. He it was who

was to bowl to me when I got to the crease.

My legs wobbled when I saw the thickset, padded-up figure of George Hirst, my batting partner, sauntering over to intercept me and I realised that it was he, not Hugh Trumble, who was to be the first bogeyman I had to overcome. He came right up to me so that we stood face to face, only a foot apart. His expression was one of amazement. 'Who the hell are *you*!' he said.

I leapt in at once and hissed at him, in an undertone: 'Lord Hawke says Play On!' With that I left him, strode to the wicket and busied myself taking guard. A legend grew up that the words spoken at this brief, but historic confrontation had been: 'We'll get 'em in singles!'

I stood in my ground, bat pointing to the heavens, and casually glanced round, taking note of the fielding positions—for all the world as if I had been doing it, season after season, in front of many thousands of people, ever since my voice had broken. I heard the umpire call out 'One to come!' and was profoundly thankful. The close-in field crouched menacingly, and there was an abatement of the deep humming from the encircling crowd of spectators.

The gaunt figure of Trumble loped up to the wicket and bowled a well-pitched-up ball. I reached forward, met it in the meaty middle of a correctly angled bat and it dropped safely in front of me. A feeling of wild relief and well-being swept over me. Perhaps I would not be called upon to face another ball. George Hirst could knock off the fifteen runs and he could shield me from the bowling—White Beard had said that he was a pastmaster at shielding a less experienced partner from hostile bowling, and I had seen him do just that when batting with Lockwood. However, I knew that if I did have to face a few more balls—say, one or two— it would be necessary for me to make a good showing, in case Doctor Redthorn entertained any suspicions that I was an impostor.

The field changed over. I glanced at George Hirst and was disconcerted to see that he was staring hard at me. Poor devil, I thought—he must be in the same state of bewilderment that I had been in for the past forty-five minutes—ever since I had walked into the Club Secretary's office and found all eyes scrutinizing me. At least I now knew what was happening. Hirst didn't have the remotest idea. He must be thinking the world had gone mad.

It was not Saunders, but Noble who was to bowl the next over to Hirst, and, while he was pacing out his run-up, I lectured myself about backing up. I must concentrate and listen for my partner's calls. I had had some dire experiences at home in Bairnsdale, running myself out and, what was far worse —almost a hanging offence—running my partner out. I grounded my bat behind the crease, flexed my legs and was keyed up to go.

It was as well I was ready because Noble's first ball was pushed wide of close-in cover and Hirst called sharply—'ONE!'—and I bolted down the wicket.

As I pulled up I was surprised to hear a great roar from the crowd; it was only when I saw my partner give a modest wave of the bat in the approved fashion that it dawned on me that he had reached his fifty. An emotional wave of admiration rolled over me. I might be a renegade Australian but I could appreciate a gritty, fighting, rearguard innings, so I stuck my bat under my arm and banged my gloved hands together in company with the Aussie fielders. It was what Wilfred Rhodes would have done, unless he were an awfully cold fish. It struck me that had I foozled that solitary ball I had received from Trumble, George Hirst would not be standing there, enjoying the ovation.

The noise subsided. Now I was at the batting end and had to forget about ovations, concentrate my mind and face the bowling of Noble, classified as a medium-pacer. Yes, a medium-pacer in first-class cricket but, to me, a club cricketer, that ball he had just bowled to Hirst had seemed like a rocket. I must keep bat and pad together—three slips and gulley were crouched, breathing down my neck.

Noble ran up with swift, smooth strides. The ball scorched down at me and hardly had I raised my bat than I felt it nick the outside edge. I jerked my head back over my right shoulder and glimpsed the slips in disarray, all lunging. It took a second or two for me to realise that the ball had flown past second slip's cap to the boundary. I had scored four runs—wonder of wonders! No credit to me, but no matter.

The four remaining balls of the over were all nightmares in their own way. The first was a yorker that struck my left boot. I felt a searing pain in my big toe and hopped about and stamped my foot on the ground. I nearly swore an Australian oath. I had no idea where the ball had gone and whether a run had gone begging. I saw Hirst—when the ball was dead—take a few steps up the pitch to me, so rather than run the risk of another confrontation with him I took up my stance at the crease, defied the painful toe and that prompted everyone to go back to their positions.

I was still wincing when I got the second ball. I tried to get my bat out of the way but I got an edge—a thin one this time. I looked back in time to see it drop out of Warwick Armstrong's left hand. It had bisected Armstrong and the 'keeper, and it had to be judged an awfully difficult chance. I breathed again.

The third ball reared up and terrified the life out of me. I got my bat up but the ball hit me on the back of the wrist, dropped and fell between my leg and the flap of my pad. As I fished it out and tossed it to the 'keeper, did I actually grin? I should have liked an adjournment for a few minutes so that I might have alternatively stamped my foot and rubbed my sore wrist, but it was not an option—Noble was moving smoothly in for the kill. My character was about to be searched again.

The last ball of that torrid over I played forward to but failed to connect—it went clean through and must have shaved the leg-stump. The crowd gasped, fearing that a bail might have been dislodged. 'AAAaaaaah!' It was uncanny. They were living every moment of it alongside me. The whole drama of life was compressed into that seething arena, and only the six grey gas-holders that brooded over the ground were indifferent. I glanced back and there was my right toe securely anchored behind the crease. I may not have connected with the ball, but I had gone through the motions of playing it correctly. Could a young, highly-tried amateur do more?

The field briskly changed over and Trumble bowled to Hirst. He dabbed at the ball—I heard him call 'ONE!' and catapulted forward. Now I was angry. What had happened to the pastmaster of the art of shielding the bowling from the more inexperienced player? Talk about 'farming' the bowling. He simply didn't believe in it. I had to face another five deliveries while he leaned on his bat.

I thumped my bat into the mark I had

made. Six or seven thumps relieved my feelings. I settled down. Trumble loped up and bowled. It was a straight and well-pitched-up ball and, although I felt afterwards I could have driven it, I played limply forward and it came to rest a few feet in front of me, swooped on by a fielder. I made up my mind that if I got an identical delivery I would drive it; Trumble, being so tall, might not be able to get down quickly enough to stop it shooting past him to the long-off boundary. (What a fool I was to think that the great Hugh Trumble would bowl two consecutive balls alike.)

What I thought was an identical delivery came down and I went to drive. I failed to connect properly and it cocked up dangerously. Trumble jack-knifed, strained forward to reach it and missed it by inches. 'AAAaaaaah!' Twenty thousand hearts stopped beating for an instant.

The next ball was a yorker. I stabbed down on it and mercifully kept it out. The next two were short, breaking away sharply to leg, but I wouldn't be tempted to go for any kind of pull shot. I knew I was at that stage in my duels with the two bowlers when they were setting out to tempt me and, if that failed, to intimidate me. It crossed my mind, as the field crossed, that the Aussie captain might bring Saunders back into the attack. A shudder ran through me at the thought. He was the fast-bowling spearhead of the attack. He had been savaged and demoralised by Jessop, and had been taken off and replaced by Monty Noble. I did not want to see him back, gunning for me.

In the next over, to my amazement, Hirst, for the third successive time, took a scurried single off the first delivery, leaving me to face the rest. If it hadn't been for the gravity of the situation I should have thought it funny, and I should have made an ironic bow in Hirst's direction. I certainly faced Noble with trepidation, remembering the last ball I had had from him, the one that had gone straight through me. I had to watch for the ball that swung into me, aiming to go through the gate.

I played the first two in classic style and, perhaps, played them so well that the bowler got annoyed and tried a couple of bouncers, but my wicket stayed intact. Provided the lightning ducking of my head was not going to rick my neck, I would stay intact as well. Had the bowler known that I have an aversion to playing the hook shot he would not have wasted two missiles from his armoury. I will say again that Noble was a medium-pacer, but he was undoubtedly bowling flat out, and it must be borne in mind that I was only a useful club cricketer who had not touched a bat for six months, batting in a poorish light on a wearing pitch—to say nothing of being encircled by a frenzied crowd. I was batting to hold my end up. As I saw it, it was my partner's responsibility to advance the score.

In the next over—Trumble bowling to Hirst—he took his single *again*—but this time off the second ball of the over. So I faced the third ball and it was a shooter, at which I played and inevitably made no contact. The crowd gasped. It was my second stump-shaver, but I believe Hirst would not have fared any better with such a treacherous delivery. Unexpectedly, I got a single off the next ball, poking at and touching one that veered away to leg. When I got to the other end I saw that Hirst had put a firm hand up. I had thought there might have been two in it but my vastly experienced partner was taking no risks of a run-out. His vetoing a second run was the first thing he had done that I approved of.

The next ball Hirst met so sweetly in the middle that mid-on failed to gather it—it really sped from the bat. We started to run and I made my ground easily. Fortuitously, there were two in it. The fielder had thrown wildly to the 'keeper but it never reached him, deflecting off Hirst's shoulder and running twenty yards or so behind the slips. I was surprised to see a grin—almost a laugh—on my partner's face as we crossed. The last ball of the over was neatly dabbed away for a quick single and I was not un-happy about that. It was the first time Hirst had deliberately shielded me from the bowl-ing. It was a luxury.

Before Noble was permitted to run up, however, Hirst embarked upon a series of preparatory acts. Perhaps he wanted to break the bowler's rhythm. He took a new guard. He surveyed the field placings, standing and pointing his bat heavenwards as if he had just arrived at the crease. He stared at the score-board, after which he made a signal to me, showing three fingers. I had not troubled with the scoreboard because I had never been sure what total we were aiming for, and I had not been keeping a tally of the runs we had scored since I had come in. His signal I interpreted as meaning that we were within three runs of victory. The crowd knew it well enough and their excitement was at fever-pitch.

Lastly, Hirst stared at the sky and, at that moment, I felt a few spots of rain on my cheek. The clouds were low and leaden in colour, and I guessed it might be raining in earnest in five or ten minutes. Looking at it realistically, however, I could not see play being abandoned at this stage of the game, with three runs wanted for victory, unless a downpour of monsoon proportions descended upon the ground. The crowd would never have stood for it. There would have been a riot.

Hirst indicated that he was ready. Four balls were bowled in a pretty negative line, outside the leg stump. The batsman was not having any. His method was strictly defensive and there was no daylight to be seen between his bat and his body. He was waiting, with true Yorkshire patience, for the ball that could be struck safely. The fifth was a faster ball, wide outside the off. Hirst stared challengingly at the umpire, but no wide was signalled. Before the last ball was bowled Noble and his skipper stood, hugger-mugger, for a time; after which a wave of the skipper's arm brought fielders closer in.

Noble bowled a well-pitched-up ball and

Hirst went to drive with his minimal back-lift. He played at it a shade too early. Noble leapt up, his fingers straining, but he failed to reach it. At the same time, mid-on tore across, dived and got it into his hands *at first bounce.* I did not have a clear view of the escape, as Hirst and I were scampering a single. The crowd, not unnaturally, thought it was a clean catch and that awful groan chilled the air—followed by an ecstatic roar of relief when they saw that the umpire's hands remained clasped behind his back. Three runs for victory had been cut to two runs for victory. I stood, vastly contented, at the non-striker's end once again. That was the end for me.

It was now raining, but not heavily. My view of the matter now was that it was all up to my partner. It rested with him. Surely, with the fielders pressing in so closely, it would be a simple matter for him to pierce the field and we could run an easy two for victory? I saw, out of the corner of my eye, that the crowd, wild with excitement, were encroaching upon the arena. Figures of small boys were darting forward and darting back.

· With the rain falling Hirst dispensed with elaborate precautions. Now, the very last thing I wanted him to do was to push at the first ball and call for a single. He pushed. I heard him call 'ONE!' *I could not believe it*! He had done precisely what I had dreaded. As I set off to run I felt the strength drain out of my legs. The crowd noise battered my ear-drums.

As I pulled up, after gaining the crease, I saw the figure of a spectator hurtling towards the middle. He came to within twenty yards of the wicket and then he was headed off by a couple of fielders who grabbed him round the waist. To my amazement I saw that he sported a dog-collar. It was a clergyman! Of course, I thought—that single has drawn us level. He thinks the winning hit has been made.

Drawn us level. *Us? Us?* What am I saying? The old, nagging uncertainty about my identity, and the ethics of my playing for

England against my native land, returned to plague me. I had to accept, now that we had run that single, Hirst and I—that the drama had been so contrived that the knife had found its way into my hand, and it was I who was called upon to strike with it. I had to strike at my own blood-brothers.

Suddenly there was George Hirst, right at my elbow. He had walked up the pitch while I had been watching the clergyman being led away. 'What's going on then?'

A surge of irritation swept over me. What a time to choose for explanations. 'Lord Hawke says Play on!' I hissed at him, as before—and added: 'Don't breathe a *word*!'

I saw his eyes blinking at me. I gazed all around me, trying to convey that we had to get on with the game. Perhaps, with rain-water trickling down my cheek like tears, I presented a pathetic spectacle. Mercifully, he at last turned and shuffled his way back to his end.

Now, in my view, Hirst, batting at No 8—having made 43 in the first innings and standing unbeaten with 58 to his credit in the second—ought to have chanced his arm with a drive or a pull. (I did not know then that chancing one's arm was not the Yorkshire way of meeting a crisis.) He had left me, yet again, with five balls to deal with. Hang it all! I had done everything Holmes had wanted. I had suffered my chin to be shaved. I had donned shirt, sweater, pads and gloves and walked, with as much *sang-froid* as I could muster, to the very rim of the volcano and faced five overs of Test-class bowling. Holmes had said not a word about going out to win the game for England. He was only concerned with the success of his stratagem.

I took up my guard. The gaunt, remorseless figure of Trumble ran up to bowl. It was a full toss that came so quickly to me I was content to see it right on to my bat, left wrist limp. The fielders uncoiled, vastly disappointed.

The next ball broke a huge distance and went harmlessly to the 'keeper on the leg side.

The next I looked at too long and came down very late on. It occurred to me I was in danger of making the same mistake Lockwood had made—allowing himself to be forced back on the right foot, seeking the advantage of being able to look for the turn of the ball. I gritted my teeth. It had to be forward play when in doubt. I dreaded the thump of the ball on the left pad and the screamed appeals for leg before.

A fleet-footed twelfth man had run on to the field and deposited a double handful of sawdust just where Trumble started his run up. Trumble took half a minute to attempt to dry the ball. Not to be outdone I rubbed and dried my glove-palms on my trousers. Inside my gloves my hands were sweating but that mattered little.

Trumble was ready to bowl. He pitched one well up to me. I was leaning forward like the prow of a ship, resolved to play forward whatever happened. *This was the ball for it.* I drove it in the direction of mid-on, but a touch wide of his right hand. He would not reach it. I started running.

As Hirst and I crossed he shouted to me but the words were lost in the inferno of noise from all round the ground. As I reached the crease the umpire put his hand on my back and urged me forward. It took me a second or two to realise he was urging me to run for the pavilion so as to escape being engulfed by the spectators, now flooding all over the playing area.

CHAPTER SEVEN

We ran awkwardly, the umpire and I, in a sort of shuffling tandem—he because he was an elderly man, and I because I was hampered by the heavy pads I wore. Eventually we were brought to a halt. We were twenty yards from the pavilion steps and it was like hacking a path through the Brazilian jungle. Hands were grasping for me. I tried to fend them off—it was no use—I was lifted clean off my feet and chaired. Hearty slaps struck my back. I had to endure it.

To my dismay I saw that I was being borne away from the pavilion steps. The chairers, and the great mass of people seemingly glued round them, had somehow to let off steam, and I was to be the means of them doing it. Shouts of 'Good old Rhodes!'—

191

'Bravo!'—'Well played!'—and 'Yorkshire forever!' reached my ears. Somebody started up 'For he's a jolly good fellow', and it was taken up by a hundred voices. I learned that day that it is a physically taxing experience to be chaired and borne along in that fashion.

At long last I was set down. Maclaren, the England captain appeared beside me, shepherded me through the crowd and bundled me up the steps and into the pavilion. I received more slaps on the back from delighted Members until we moved on and got into a private corridor. I was ready to drop.

Maclaren paused outside the door of Mr Alcock's office and said to me, in a low voice: 'Well played! That goes without saying. Look, I don't pretend to know half of what's been going on, but I know one thing for certain. If the Aussies find out about the trick we've just pulled on them it'll spell the end of Test Matches between them and us for the next twenty years.'

He squared his shoulders, tapped on the door and opened it. We stepped inside and he closed the door quietly. The day having worn on since I was last in the room, it seemed poorly lit. Mr Alcock was seated at his desk, with Lord Hawke, standing, in close attendance on his left. On his right stood Sherlock Holmes and another man, whom I took to be Doctor Denzil Redthorn. The latter, although a well-built man, stood with a slumped posture that compared unfavourably with Holmes' erect figure. I noticed that his left hand was bandaged. His face had an unhealthy high colour, his eyes dark-rimmed and unnaturally deep-set.

All eyes were directed towards me. I recalled my briefing—that I was to point a finger at Redthorn and say, accusingly: 'That's him!' I could not bring myself to do it. I had been involved in too much play-acting, poor puppet that I was. I craved some kind of respite. I had been haled from one arena to another—from one spotlight to another—from the tumult of a great sporting amphitheatre to the frightening silence of a half-lit closet scene, with scarcely a minute to catch my breath. It was too much for me. My legs buckled under me and Maclaren sprang forward to support me and save me from falling to a heap on the floor.

I felt myself being dragged a yard or two and lowered into a chair. Just at that moment I heard a voice burst out in a half-hysterical cry: 'All right, damn you! Have it your own way. I admit it. It *was* me!'

The same pocket-flask I had gulped at an hour earlier was put to my lips and tipped, as before, so that I had, perforce, to swallow two mouthfuls. I opened my eyes and saw Mr Alcock, whose face wore a concerned expression—and, beside him, Mr Holmes, tight-lipped, pale and strained as ever.

'Are you all right?' asked the dispenser of the brandy in a kindly tone. By means of a nod and a weak smile I assured him I was.

Just then I heard sounds of a scuffle over by the door. I looked and saw that Maclaren was barring the way to Doctor Redthorn, gripping his wrist. 'Mind my hand, damn you!' grated the doctor. 'You can't keep me here against my will. The police will hear of this.'

'I suggest you come away from the door.' (This was Holmes, speaking at his most authoritative.) 'You have confessed to being implicated in the mystery of Wilfred Rhodes' disappearance this morning.'

The doctor returned, crestfallen, to the centre of the office, goaded by a push in the back from the England captain.

'As I told you,' continued Holmes grimly. 'Mr Rhodes has given us only the bare out-line of the facts, not having had time to give more. He has been kept busy since he unex-pectedly, but providentially, arrived at the Oval little more than an hour ago. Now, Doctor Redthorn, we are all curious to hear you give a detailed account of what took place, and I urge you to be quite open with us. As for the police, it may or may not be in *our* best interest to call the police in to manage this affair—it will certainly not be in *your* best interest. The sooner we get to the bottom of this matter the better for all concerned. We all have other business to attend to elsewhere.'

The doctor stared at the sentinel-like figure of Maclaren at the door. 'Could I have a chair?' he muttered. There were only three chairs in the room. Mr Alcock's desk-chair, in which he sat. I, of course, was occupying one, revived by the brandy and fascinated by the drama being enacted in front of me. Holmes brought the third chair up, the doctor slumped into it and, after a long hesitation, began his account.

'I must begin by telling you, gentlemen, that things haven't gone right for me in recent months. My wife has—has temporarily left my house and taken our daughter with her. In consequence, my health has not been good, and not only my health—my practice has suffered too. Regrettably, I have resorted to—to stimulants, and things of that sort. Also I have found it necessary to take opiates, my mind being in such an unhappy state. Sleepless nights and so forth. I hope—I sincerely hope—that none of you gentlemen have any knowledge of these kinds of misfortune—I mean, knowledge born of experience. I think it unlikely. Fate has dealt harshly with me. I am, God help me, an unlucky traveller along life's...'

'We can dispense with the self-pity, Doctor Redthorn,' interjected Lord Hawke sharply.

'Self-pity!' burst out the other. 'It's all very fine for you—a peer of the realm, born with a silver spoon...'

'Denzil, that's enough of that!' Mr Alcock leaned forward over his desk and wagged a finger at the doctor.

'Nor was I born with a silver spoon in my mouth,' said Lord Hawke forcibly. 'I was born in a country parsonage and my title fell to me by a freak of chance. Your incivility is only exceeded by your ignorance.'

The doctor's emotionalism subsided. He lowered his head and rubbed the spot between his eyes. 'I am sorry. Well, I had slept badly this last night, in spite of...well, I had taken something to help me get off to sleep.

The trouble is, I now have what is called a tolerance to these things. At last I did get off, but I was roused by a loud hammering at the front door. It was insistent. I knew there was no avoiding it, so I dragged myself out of bed, put a dressing-gown on and went down. I decided that, whoever it was, and whatever the malaise, I would make them pay through the nose. With my candle I lit the gas-light in the hall, and then I opened the door. Standing in the doorway was a sight that made my blood run cold. A man stood there, his face grotesquely distorted— his teeth bared and snarling at me, it seemed, like a cornered wild animal—his tongue floundering in his wide-open mouth. Horrible sounds came from his throat.

'I tried to shut the door. He forced his way in. He was covered with perspiration and kept pointing to his lower jaw and grunting and gurgling. At last it dawned on me that he had dislocated his jaw—it sometimes happens with yawning, when somebody is dog-tired. I can tell you it was a relief to my distraught nerves when I realised I did not have a raving madman to deal with, as I had at first thought. I had no idea, of course, who he was—I had never set eyes on him before—or where he had come from. He was not dressed for a chilly morning and I guessed he had not long quitted his sleeping quarters. Well, I lit more lights and got him stretched out on the couch in my consulting-room. I attempted to get the jaw re-located, or, at least, to reduce the dislocation. As a student at the teaching hospital I had seen a demonstration of the technique, so I had some notion of how to go about it. Like a fool I rushed at it. The moment I pressed my fingers down on his back teeth there must have been a spasmodic clenching of them and I got badly bitten. He started to howl and I howled louder. A joke, perhaps, you think it, but to me it was a waking nightmare. The pain in the smaller fingers of my left hand, which had come off worst, and the tearing to shreds of my nerves, drove me into a blind fury. I thought to inject him with something to quieten him and relax the muscles in his jaw. I filled a syringe with something, I don't know what. I had dozens of phials, all in confusion. I've been experimenting with drug mixtures of late. I injected him. What dosage I'd given him I didn't know or care. I mean, I didn't care at that moment, when I was so frenzied.'

Doctor Redthorn turned his head and his eyes met mine. It was only for a second or two. He seemed to gather himself and then went on. 'I threw myself into a chair, nursing and cursing my hand. I went into the kitchen at the back of the house and made some coffee and tried to drink it black, but it only made me retch. I could keep none of it down. When I returned to look at the man on the couch he was quiet. He was too quiet, and I didn't like the look of him. However, I decided to attack the problem and put on some leather gloves. This time I proceeded with care, pressed down on the back teeth of the lower jaw and pushed the jaw backward. It worked. I had succeeded in re-locating it. But there was no joy for me. I saw that he was unconscious, his eyes pinpointed, his skin dry and cold. I knew the signs. I was afraid. What if he should die? That would be the final hammer-blow of Fate. I cursed the day my father had forced me into medicine.'

He paused and shot a baleful glance at Mr Alcock, but could not withstand the Secretary's stern and unflinching gaze. He lowered his head and we all stared at him. The only sound in that sound-proofed room was the ticking of the clock on the wall. At length he resumed his tale, half-lifting his head. 'I decided I had to get him to a hospital quickly. I was not competent—nor was I, physically, in a fit state—to deal with a probable case of—of drug poisoning. I telephoned for a cab to come to the door. A quarter of an hour later I heard a horse's hooves and I carried the dead weight of the stranger out to the kerbside. The cabbie helped me put him in the cab, and I gave instructions that he was to be taken to the Italian Hospital, less than half a mile down the road.'

'Why did you not accompany your patient to the hospital?' questioned Holmes coolly.

'I—I—it was my intention to proceed there, on foot, when I was properly dressed.'

'You had time to dress in the quarter of an hour you waited for the cab.'

'I was occupied all that time trying to revive him,' protested the doctor.

'You were occupied all that time—I will concede that,' said Holmes, now placing himself directly before the seated man. 'You say you carried the stranger out to the kerbside. You omit to mention that you had discovered that he was Wilfred Rhodes, the famous Yorkshire cricketer. You had been through his pockets. You say that you telephoned for a cab to come to the door of your house. In fact, however, you telephoned for a cab to go to the door of Doctor Gupta's house in Swancombe Gardens, the garden of which backs on to the garden of your house. You believed that Doctor Gupta was, like yourself, connected to the telephone, but in that you were mistaken, because Doctor Gupta had his telephone disconnected a week ago. You see the truth of the adage: what a tangled web we weave, when we practise to deceive. So why did you set out to deceive? Because you had formed the diabolical plan of attempting to implicate Doctor Gupta and blacken his reputation, of which you were jealous. You resented his coming into the district and prospering—to the detriment, you supposed, of your own practice, although it is most likely that your practice suffered as a result of your neglect and mismanagement of it.

'In the quarter of an hour you waited for the cab to arrive at Doctor Gupta's house you were very busy. You darkened your face with some substance—perhaps a mixture of soot and oil—put on a large cape-coat and a hat with a wide brim and put your patient over your shoulder. You made your way down to the bottom of your garden and gained entry to Doctor Gupta's garden by way of an interjacent alleyway, leaving there at least one extra deep footmark in a patch of soft earth. You arrived at the front of his house just as the cab drew up. You spoke to the cabbie with an assumed accent, designed to convince him that you were an Indian, and I may tell you that you succeeded well in that. You also deceived him into thinking that you intended to accompany your patient to the hospital—you feared he might be disinclined to make the journey on his own. When his back was turned you seized the opportunity of stealing out of the cab—it was still dark and you were able to escape his notice. Do you deny any of this?'

The accused man's head had sunk lower and lower as Holmes set out the items in the indictment. No word came from him, nor any shake or nod of his head.

'Later in the morning,' Holmes continued, 'you gloated over the scheme you had devised to incriminate your rival, but you were not satisfied. You wondered if it might be possible to incriminate him further. You took a pair of scissors and cut words from a thesaurus and pasted them on to a slip of paper. It was a message to the Club Secretary, the composition of which you foolishly imagined to be brilliantly clever. The wording was what you supposed would be natural to a simple-minded Indian who wished, anonymously, to ease his conscience by revealing the whereabouts and welfare of Wilfred Rhodes. Your estimate of Doctor Gupta was that he was racially inferior, that he lacked a proper command of the English language, and that, when he addressed or referred to men with white skins, he did so obsequiously, giving them the title of ''sahib''.

'My guess is that, at first, you intended to direct Mr Alcock to the Italian Hospital, naming it in full, but that you eliminated the word ''Hospital'' from the message. Why? Because your constant fear was that Wilfred Rhodes might be dying, and that, if he were, and the police got to his bedside quickly, they might learn that you were responsible for his condition. You wanted the police to act, but not too swiftly. You imagined a situation, after Rhodes' death, in which a police investigation could link the message to evidence given by the cabbie who took the unconscious Rhodes to the Italian Hospital. It would all point to Doctor Gupta. You would not be implicated, and you would be revenged on the rival practitioner. I can tell you that Doctor Gupta, whom I presume you have never met or spoken to, is far from having a weak grasp of English. It was your foolishness that exposed your villainy. You are your own betrayer in this affair, and I suggest that you are not so much an unlucky traveller along life's highway, as you wish to represent yourself, but an unscrupulous and cowardly one, and I, for one, rejoice to see you crushed—and your evil hopes turned to dust and ashes.'

These were darts too piercing to be borne passively by the man at whom they were aimed. He sprang up from his chair and threw himself towards the door. Maclaren once again sought to restrain him, but a sharp command came from Lord Hawke. 'Let him go, Maclaren!' The England captain stood back and Doctor Redthorn made an abrupt exit. At this juncture Mr Alcock calmly began removing my boots and pads. What a relief it was to get out of the cricket gear and put on my proper clothes.

'Redthorn is right. We cannot keep him,' said Lord Hawke, coming forward from behind the desk to confront Sherlock Holmes. 'Those were hard words you spoke, Mr Holmes.'

'Would you have used softer ones, my lord?'

'No, indeed.' (This was said in a low tone.) His lordship continued: 'Mr Holmes, I mean to keep in reserve my congratulations on the skill and assiduity with which you have conducted your investigation of this mystery. First, I must ask you this. Is it a fact that, at the time you came to sit with the Club Secretary and myself in the

Members' Stand, you knew that Wilfred Rhodes was a patient in the Italian Hospital in Bloomsbury?'

'I cannot deny it, my lord.'

'So you deliberately deceived us. We agreed to the stratagem you proposed only because you persuaded us that there was no other way we might discover his whereabouts. Yet you knew where he was all the time. Have you any idea of the risks we ran when we engaged in this mad escapade— the risks we are still running. What is going to happen when—?'

Holmes had the temerity to interrupt at this point. 'Risks? Oh, come now! You will, I trust, allow me to point out that, for a quarter of London's four million inhabitants, being born, and remaining alive, is sufficiently risky. This sporting arena is only a millionth part of the whole metropolis, and the dramas enacted here, so far as I am concerned, are quite without significance. For the people of Poplar and Limehouse the dramas are real, and the question at issue is whether families are to live or die, in the face of starvation and disease—not whether men in white flannels are to win or lose a cricket match. You will, I trust, forgive me for speaking frankly.'

Lord Hawke blinked. It took him some time to recover his aplomb. 'I perceive, Mr Holmes,' he said grimly, 'that you are a Radical.'

Holmes smiled and replied genially: 'I would be obliged if you would not attach a label to me. I take no interest in politics.'

'And I perceive also that your opinion of cricketers is in line with that of Mr Rudyard Kipling, who calls them "flannelled fools".'

Holmes seemed now to be relishing the exchange. 'Oh, indeed, I should have said my opinion leaned that way, my lord, had I not recently made the acquaintance of my young assistant here.' He turned to me and smiled. 'In him, at least, I have not so far detected any signs of foolishness.'

'Yes,' said Lord Hawke, favouring me with a look, and I recalled the moment when I had first set foot inside the office, and his lordship had stared at me and restricted himself to saying no more than 'Yes.'

'When I talk of running risks, Mr Holmes, I have in mind certain inquisitive gentlemen of the press. This morning it was given out to them that Wilfred Rhodes was indisposed and would miss the early morning's play—but, it was to be hoped, would recover in time to play his part in the fourth innings of the match. The dramatic outcome of the game, and the part Rhodes, supposedly, played in it, will have gingered up their curiosity about his indisposition, and questions attaching to it. When did he recover? What time did he get to the Oval? Was he suffering any discomfort when he went out to bat? You do see that we are not out of the wood yet?'

Sherlock Holmes nodded. He then moved swiftly to the desk and lifted the receiver of the telephone. 'More important than that—I believe I can get the latest word on Wilfred

Rhodes' condition.'

A few minutes later he was speaking to Doctor Bartoli and enquiring after the patient. We judged from several exclamations from Holmes—one of 'Excellent!' and one of 'Capital!'—that the news was cheerful. Towards the end of the conversation we heard him enquire whether Rhodes was strong enough to endure visits from 'relatives and friends'. It seemed, from his final exclamation of 'Splendid!' that he was.

'He is vastly improved,' Holmes repeated, replacing the receiver. 'He is taking nourishment and will be fit enough to be discharged the day after tomorrow—Friday. Doctor Bartoli says the patient has an iron constitution.'

Lord Hawke announced that he would go to visit him within the hour. He then requested the four of us—Maclaren, Alcock, Holmes and myself—to call at his room in Jermyn Street on the morrow at 2.30 in the afternoon. He himself would arrange that George Hirst would also be in attendance, if he deemed it necessary. Thus would be gathered together the six members of the conspiracy. A course of action would then be decided upon. We all, separately and solemnly, promised to attend. I acquiesced with a nod.

'One last thing, my lord,' said Holmes, as Lord Hawke moved towards the door. 'You spoke of risks a little while ago, and of your fears that the gentlemen of the press might be lurking, unduly inquisitive. I have one last conjuring trick to perform.' He dug into his capacious coat pocket, took out several hairy objects, not instantly identifiable—put them on the desk and examined each in turn.

'Ah, this one, I think. It seems to answer the purpose.' It was a false beard and, when he had fitted it to my chin, it was held *in situ* by means of an elastic band running over the crown of my head and concealed under my hair.

'*Voilà!*' said Holmes. 'Wilfred Rhodes is not here. What happened to him? He stole away—sensible fellow!—almost immediately after the match finished, wishing to avoid the fuss and commotion—still a little indisposed. Has he gone to his lodging or directly to the railway terminus to catch his train for the North? We have no means of knowing. As for myself, a guest of the Chairman of the Board of Selectors, I arrived with my young Australian assistant, bearded like the pard—and now I am leaving with him.'

Mr Alcock smiled at the restoration of my bearded appearance, and I expected a nod of approval from Lord Hawke; he, however, was staring at Holmes, a look of consternation on his face. '*Australian*! Did I hear you say *Australian*?'

It shot through my mind that Holmes had, inadvertently, let that dreaded word slip out. Now the fat was in the fire.

Holmes was equal to the emergency. 'No, no, my lord—you heard me describe my young assistant as *très lion*—a French phrase, meaning—having the qualities of a lion. I was brought up partly in France. No, no, no, he is not an Australian—he is the nephew of the Bishop of Tewkesbury, an old college friend of mine.'

Lord Hawke muttered something unintelligible, turned and made his exit, with Maclaren following.

Mr Alcock had put cricket bat, batting pads and batting gloves back into Rhodes' cricket bag and snapped it shut. I should like to have had a last swish with that bat—a last feel of the handle between my hands—before it disappeared from view.

'Mr Holmes, you will want to leave now. It will be better if you do not attract any attention, and so I will see you out of the ground. I'll guide you, by way of the kitchen, to a door at the rear, used by tradesmen. Getting a hansom will not prove easy, I fear. Have you thought of that?'

Holmes was buttoning his coat. 'Oh, we shall walk back to Westminster Bridge. A breath of fresh air will do my young assistant a power of good.'

And so we quitted the office, between whose four walls so much that was truly bizarre had happened that day in August, 1902.

We made our way along a corridor. Suddenly, from around a corner, a man appeared and stood in our path. We halted.

'I say, Secretary, where have you been hiding?' The questioner was a jovial-looking man of middle age, inclined to fleshiness. I admired the plum-coloured waistcoat he wore.

'I am not aware that I have been hiding anywhere,' replied Mr Alcock stiffly. He did not seem pleased at the unexpected encounter.

'Thought you'd be where the champagne's been flowing—in the dressing-room. What about the mighty Jessop then, eh? The eighth wonder of the world, what? Who said English cricket is on the slide? You see me hatless. I threw my hat away when young Rhodes hit the winning run. It isn't like me to let myself get carried away.' He beamed at us, and seemed quite proud of having committed the reckless act of throwing his hat away.

'Isn't it just another working day for you scribblers?'

'What? More like a Roman holiday—with the Aussies thrown to the lions. I have to watch some pretty humdrum stuff in the course of my work. It isn't a bed of roses, being cooped up in a stuffy press box all day.'

'I hope you are not complaining about—'

'Heavens, no. Thanks entirely to you, Secretary, the press box at the Oval is the best in the country. Have you seen the one at Trent Bridge? It's just a wooden shanty. In any case, if I wanted to complain about the facilities here I should not be so discourteous as to do it before strangers. I don't think I've met—er—'

It was clear that the jovial pressman did not intend the encounter to be a brief one. Mr Alcock had no choice. 'This is Mr Holmes. He is in rather a hurry—'

'Would that be Mr Sherlock Holmes, the Baker Street detective?'

'As a matter of fact, it would.'

'I saw you from the press box,' said the pressman, looking at Holmes with an artful smile playing about his lips. 'You were sitting with Lord Hawke. I must say his lordship seemed quite entranced by your conversation—so entranced, in fact, that he scarcely looked at the cricket. I thought that very singular. And, some time later, the three of you turned your back on the cricket and retreated into the pavilion, didn't you? Oh, some compelling reason, I dare say— some necessary business. None of my concern, eh?'

'As to that, I would not disagree with you,' said Mr Alcock, growing more impatient every minute. 'Now if you will excuse us—'

'I say, I've been scouting round for one of the heroes of the hour, Wilfred Rhodes. I'd like to get a quote from him. He's a man of few words, but those few words are usually well worth printing. Dashed if I can locate him, and nobody I've spoken to seems to have any idea what happened to him. Can't get anything out of Maclaren, whom I ran into a moment ago.'

'I believe he changed and went off in something of a rush to catch his train,' said Mr Alcock.

'What—left the ground already?'

'I believe so.'

'I say, that's deuced odd. George Hirst is still here, and they usually travel together. Quite inseparable.' He turned to Holmes, behind whose back I was skulking, feeling self-conscious with the false beard on my chin. 'Mr Holmes, I've got a four-wheeler carriage and pair outside, courtesy of the almanack—one of the "perks" of the job. Can I give you a lift anywhere? You won't find it easy to get a hansom.'

Holmes bowed to him. 'That is a very kind offer, Mr—er—'

Reluctantly, Mr Alcock had, perforce, to make a belated introduction. 'This is Mr

Caine, of Wisden's cricketers' almanack.'

'Charles Stewart Caine, if you please. My mother was a Scotswoman, and brought me up to insist upon my name being given in full—particularly the *Stewart* part.' He beamed as if this was a great sally of wit. He had dimples in his cheeks—possibly the products of his excessive joviality.

Holmes shook his proffered hand, introduced me briefly as 'a young friend of mine', and said he was grateful for the offer of a lift and would accept it. This development quite staggered me and, judging by the glazed expression on Mr Alcock's face, it staggered him even more. However, thus it was to be, and thus it was that we took our leave of the guide who had attempted to lead us away from the enemy's main positions, but had, unluckily, led us straight to an enemy patrol on reconnaissance.

Outside it was drizzling still. Most of the huge crowd that had built up for the climax of the match had, by this time, got clear of the immediate area and were bound for home and five o'clock tea. Yet still the streets were jammed with wheeled traffic of all kinds, and clogged by hundreds of people edging along on foot.

We had not far to walk to Caine's four-wheeler—a handsome vehicle, drawn by two fine horses. 'My place is in St John's Wood,' said Caine nonchalantly. 'Shall I drop you off in Baker Street?'

Holmes had not done with amazing me. He requested that we be dropped off at 'the boarding-house where my young friend is staying', and gave the address as 6, Eversley Gardens in Bloomsbury. I had to search back in my memory in order to identify this address. It was, I remembered, the address of the boarding-house where Wilfred Rhodes was staying. We had never had cause to visit it during our investigation of the Rhodes mystery.

'As you wish,' said Caine amiably. 'It will call for a detour, but a trifling one.'

We climbed into the roomy interior of the carriage, Holmes and I occupying the rear seat, while Caine sat opposite with his back to the coachman. A whip cracked and we lurched into motion. Caine peered out of the window at the masses of people surging along the pavement.

'I say, I wonder which one of these blighters picked up my hat and laid claim to it.'

'Possession is nine-tenths of the law, isn't it?' said Holmes dryly.

'Do you know, I bought that hat in Austin Reed's for twenty-two and sixpence. I was attached to it. Or, perhaps I should say that, when I wore it, it was attached to me.' He laughed jovially, and Holmes smiled to acknowledge the joke. I could not have smiled because I was so uneasy about the situation we were in. Caine suspected something, of that I was sure. 'I got so carried away when young Rhodes hit the winning run. Away went my hat. Fine cricketer, Rhodes. I've seen a lot of him in the past two years.' He smiled broadly and his eyes rested on me. I looked away. Why had Holmes walked into what might prove to be a spider's web, spun to catch two poor flies? Was I beginning to lose faith in the Great Detective?

'I think you must weary of watching cricket, week in and week out,' said Holmes.

'I weary of the travel part of it, yes,' replied Caine. 'Of course, the almanack is very good to me, and I travel first-class. I also weary of the unspeakable press boxes— I've known the time when there was no press box, as such, but only a tent, with its doorway facing into a stiff breeze.' He pursued this theme of facilities at cricket grounds up and down the country, and related a few anecdotes.

'A tedious game, cricket,' commented Holmes lazily.

Caine threw up his hands. 'Great heavens! To say such a thing on today of all days. You are indulging a sardonic vein of humour, surely? I do not deny it is sometimes tedious, but it has a surprisingly large share of madcap moments, with masquerades and mysteries.'

'Masquerades?' said Holmes. 'Why do you say masquerades?'

'Oh, I don't know,' replied Caine, with a mocking smile. 'I think I had in mind, about a decade ago, when T.C O'Brien, a stalwart of the Middlesex team, played three or four games for the county under the name of J.E Johnston, thereby concealing his true identity. His motive? Well, some said he was hiding from creditors who were dunning him. More likely, it was a practical joke.'

'Indulging a sardonic vein of humour, perhaps,' said Holmes.

'Ha, Ha! That's good. No, indulging a whimsical vein of humour is more like it. O'Brien being the son of an Irish peer. Of course, *I* saw it. *I* knew it was he. I have a sharp eye for things of that sort. It's not so easy to pull the wool over my eyes. By Jove! I should like to change places with you, Mr Holmes. I have always fancied I had some gifts in that direction.'

'What direction is that?' enquired Holmes.

'Why, sniffing around for clues. Using

one's powers of observation. I say, a man who is sought out and called upon to solve mysteries cannot know anything of ordinary, humdrum existence such as the rest of us have to endure.'

'You would be wrong to think that. A good detective must know everything of ordinary, humdrum existence.'

'Of course, I believe there are mysteries all around us, at all times,' continued Caine, and he now seemed to be selecting his words more carefully. 'Mysteries—some trifling, and some not so trifling—which may be solved by keeping one's eyes and ears open. Take, as an example, what I consider to be a mystery—perhaps a trifling one—namely, the non-appearance of Wilfred Rhodes this morning. Oh yes, we were told he was indisposed. Do you know, it is curious how a certain number keeps recurring in this little mystery. Number eleven. Firstly, that is the number of Rhodes' position in the batting order—although, undoubtedly, he is worthy of a higher position. Next, there are the eleven mysterious words written on the note that was delivered to the Club Secretary just before the match began.'

There was a tense hiatus.

'Oh, you mean the little note he received,' said Holmes. 'How do you come to know about that?'

Caine rubbed his finger beside his nose. 'Shall we say—by means of a little detective work? I had heard somebody say that one of the stewards had taken a note to the Secretary. I was curious, so I located the steward and put a few questions to him. The note had been passed to him, he said, by an urchin who had then run off. He told me that when the Secretary took the note and read it, his comment was: "This is brief enough. Only eleven words—and God knows what I am to make of it." '

'The steward did not himself read the note, I take it.'

'No—I wish he had. I am very curious as to what might have been in that note. Later, when I learned that Rhodes had not put in an appearance, I wondered if the note had anything to do with it.'

'I cannot see why you should think there might be a connection,' said Holmes.

'I think the idea of a connection had, indeed, begun to fade from my mind—but it was revived when I happened to look down from my little eyrie and saw you in hugger-mugger with Lord Hawke and the Secretary, the recipient of the note. Clearly, you were discussing something of great importance—something that took priority over the cricket. Who would have thought that the attention of the Chairman of the Board of Selectors could have been so easily distracted? Unlike his lordship, however, I could not afford to give the cricket a miss—a good reporter must keep his eye on the game, watch every ball and be constantly jotting things down. It was a colleague who told me he had seen you go back into the pavilion. My colleague was only mildly interested, but I was more than mildly interested. As I say, it revived my feeling that there was something going on behind the scenes. Lo and behold, at the fall of Lilley's wicket, who should appear—after an unusually long wait—and walk, quite unscathed, to the wicket—but Wilfred Rhodes himself.'

'You talk of solving a mystery, Mr Caine,' said Holmes calmly, 'but it seems to me you are attempting to create a mystery where none exists. Rhodes was indisposed in the morning, but he rallied in the afternoon and made haste to the Oval so that he might honour his contract to play. Where is the mystery?'

'I mean to tell you where the mystery is, never fear. You were surprised that I knew about that note, weren't you? I have more surprises for you. For instance, would it surprise you to know that I could tell you precisely where Wilfred Rhodes is at this very moment?'

'At this very moment, Mr Caine?'

'At this very moment, Mr Holmes.'

Holmes said nothing. He turned and peered out of the window, rubbing some of the condensation away with his gloved hand so as to make a little spyhole. He unbuttoned his coat and took out his watch. Was this merely a piece of theatrical business, or was he, perhaps, logging the stages of our journey. Why should he do that? I only felt numb with foreboding.

He turned back to face Caine. 'Oh, I doubt if you could tell me that. Your little detective work, as you call it, has not gone deep enough. The cobbler should stick to his last, as the saying goes—and I would advise you to stick to cricket reporting.'

Caine leaned right forward and the smile that had been constantly on his lips began to turn sour. 'Are you trying to make a fool of me? Don't be too sure that I can't turn the tables on you and make a fool of you instead. That would be quite a feat, wouldn't it? I wonder if anyone has ever beaten you at your own game.'

Holmes slowly returned his watch to his fob-pocket. As he did so his fingers closed over the sovereign that was linked to his watch-chain. I remembered his telling me that it had been given to him by a woman—the only person who had ever beaten him. Irene Adler—wasn't that her name? And was he within an inch of being beaten again?

Caine's hand suddenly reached forward. He grasped my false beard and wrenched it off. I felt the cool air on my exposed chin. 'He is in this four-wheeler, Mr Clever Sherlock Holmes—that is where Wilfred Rhodes is at this very moment—sitting beside you.'

He lay back in his seat, his face suffused with a glow of satisfaction and wreathed with a smile of triumph. Seconds ticked away, and they seemed long seconds. Then he leaned forward and tossed the false beard into Holmes' lap. It was close to being a contemptuous gesture. 'Your property, I imagine. I hope I've not damaged it.'

Holmes turned to me—those deep-sunken eyes bored into mine. 'I advise you not to say anything, Mr Rhodes. Leave me to deal with it.'

'So you see I have not attempted to create

a mystery. I have uncovered one, have I not?' Caine, obviously, savoured every sweet word of his taunt.

'Indeed you have. You have taken me aback, I must confess. I underestimated you. I owe you an apology. Perhaps, if you give me leave, it shall be in the form of a full explanation of what has occurred today, as it concerns Mr Rhodes. He, by the way, is not at all a well man.'

'I am all ears,' said the smirking Caine.

'The truth of the matter is—' began Holmes.

'I am glad we are to have the truth at last,' interrupted Caine. I fought to conceal my anger at this. That he should speak so insolently to the Great Detective was something hardly to be borne.

'The truth is—' continued Holmes calmly, '—that when Mr Rhodes returned to his room at the boarding-house yesterday evening he found a letter waiting for him, written and posted the day before. It was from a lady to whom he was engaged to be married. The marriage was to have taken place next month. The letter was not only to tell him the engagement was broken off, but that she was only hours away from sailing to America with a man whom Rhodes had, for many years, regarded as a close and trusted friend.

'You can imagine his feelings when he read that letter. It was blacker news than any he could expect to hear, even should he live to be a hundred. It was a bolt out of the blue, for he had had no suspicion that anything was amiss. He retired to bed, but could not sleep. I am telling this tale, just as he told it to me in Kennington Park.'

'Kennington Park—what has that to do with it?' said Caine.

'Forgive me—I am running on ahead of myself.' He glanced out of the spyhole in the window for a few seconds. 'He could not sleep. In the early hours, before dawn, he rose and quitted the house. He started upon a wandering, not only of his steps, but also of his mind, so distressed was he. He found his way down to the Thames Embankment, where he was, perhaps, scarcely distinguishable—because of his dejected appearance—from the unfortunates who, nightly, sleep on the benches there. As the morning wore on he collected his wits sufficiently to make his way to the Oval on foot, wrote a few words on a slip of paper and gave an urchin a halfpenny to take it to the turnstiles. He did not show himself. In this way it eventually reached the Club Secretary. The note read: *Cannot play today so unhappy she brought me to this Rhodes.* Just eleven words. Mysterious you called them, Mr Caine. Mysterious they seemed to the Club Secretary.'

CHAPTER EIGHT

Holmes had told this pack of lies in such an untypically quiet and melting tone of voice that, to my surprise, I found myself affected by his words and the picture it conjured in my mind. I felt a pricking of the eyes and felt the need to rub them with my fingertips. It occurred to me that Caine might be watching me do this. I blinked in his direction and saw him eyeing me.

'You may have wondered what had brought me to the Oval,' continued Holmes. 'As a matter of fact, I take little or no interest in competitive games, and cricket I consider a waste of time. I had met Lord Hawke when staying at Sir George Barkworth's place in Lincolnshire last October. I was able to clear up a little matter of blackmail. I tell you this in confidence. Nothing ever got into the newspapers. On that occasion Lord Hawke invited me to be his guest at one of this year's Test Matches. I conveniently forgot the invitation, but his lordship inconveniently remembered it and telephoned me last night, assuring me that today's play promised to be an entertaining one and that, moreover, it would be the last opportunity to see any Test cricket in 1902. The result was that I arrived at the Oval at mid-day.

'When I arrived I was told that Rhodes had not appeared, shown the note he had sent to the Club Secretary, and asked if I could suggest a course of action. I had the germ of an idea where I might find him. It seemed to me that, after getting a message to the Secretary and wearying of tramping the streets, he might turn into the park at Kennington, which is, of course, adjacent to the cricket ground. There he could sit, rest and think. Sure enough, I found him sitting miserably on a hard park bench. It took me half an hour to persuade him that a hot

beverage might make him feel more cheerfully disposed towards life, and we adjourned
to a nearby coffee stall. We sat and talked
and I confided to him that I, too, had suffered a cruel disappointment, when a young
man, not dissimilar from the one he had suffered. I, too, had been deceived by a lady—'

'What was her name?' broke in Caine
sharply.

'Adler. Irene Adler,' replied Holmes instantly.

'Adler? Isn't that a German name?'

'She was a Viennese. A music student. She
later pursued a modest career as an opera
singer on the continent. But, to continue—I
believe Mr Rhodes was impressed by my
candour and—I think I may fairly say—my
compassion. He gradually began to view
matters in a different light and agreed to
return with me to the Oval. There I handed him over to Mr Maclaren, the England
captain. I then went down to the Members'
Stand to tell Lord Hawke and Mr Alcock
of my success in finding him and bringing

him to the ground. You saw me talking with them.'

'You had a great deal to say to them,' said Caine.

'Yes—I wanted them to understand Mr Rhodes' frame of mind. I did not want him to be badgered with questions. That would not have helped matters. Explanations could come later. Also, I told them that he had made the stipulation that, when the match was over, he was to be shielded from the press and all forms of publicity whatever. As you see, I have taken that upon my own shoulders.'

'With a false beard,' said Caine, with a measure of scorn in his voice.

'It would have deceived anybody but you, Mr Caine,' said Holmes quietly, and I marvelled that he could import so much of what seemed genuine admiration into those few words.

I became aware that Caine was staring hard at me. When Holmes had been spinning his yarn I had felt keenly the awkwardness of my position, and had been dreading the moment when Caine might speak to me. Neither Lord Hawke, nor Mr Alcock, had heard me utter a single word. Caine had boasted of having a sharp eye and had, perhaps, proved it. Doubtless he had a sharp ear too, and so I was anxious that he should not hear my Australian tones.

The moment of crisis came. 'Tell me, Mr Rhodes—what made you send that message to the Club Secretary?'

This question, I knew, was a feeler. Other more searching ones would follow. I dropped, first my eyes, then my head, and tried to assume a tongue-tied, shamefaced expression.

'Ah, here we are, if I mistake not,' said Holmes, rubbing the steamed-up window and enlarging his spyhole. 'So this is where you lodge when you come to Town.' The situation was saved. It was like a miracle. Much later, when he and I had leisure to discuss the events of the day, he told me that he had indeed made the spyhole so as to be able to log the stages of the journey. He had tailored the length of the yarn he had spun so that his finishing it should coincide with our arrival at the boarding-house. Thus no time was left for awkward questions.

The carriage came to rest by the kerb and we clambered out, all three. We had stopped outside a solid, four-storey house—evidently a boarding-house of the highest class—with double bay-windows, from which I saw a few faces peering curiously. I imagined the appearance of a handsome four-wheeler was above ordinary interest.

Holmes thanked Caine for the lift and added, with a wry smile: 'I say nothing of what I suppose to have been your ulterior motive when you offered it.'

'Oh, I say, look here,' said Caine huffily. 'Who is talking about hidden motives?'

'Perhaps you are right,' conceded Holmes. 'Well, there's no need for you to wait for me. I shall stay with Mr Rhodes for a while. When I leave for Baker Street I can easily get a cab in the Euston Road.'

The artful smile returned to play about Caine's fleshy lips. 'Oh, I'll see you to the door. I want to dispel, once and for all, the suspicions I have been entertaining. I am not at all sure that you are not still trying to pull the wool over my eyes. Don't be offended. I realise that bamboozling people is one of the arts of your profession.'

Holmes seemed affronted at this. 'I am not retained by Lord Hawke or Mr Alcock, if that is what you mean. My interest in Mr Rhodes is not professional, I assure you.'

Caine gave a hollow laugh. 'Well, you are a noble fellow, Mr Sherlock Holmes—I would not doubt it. Still, if you have no objection, I will accompany the two of you to the door to see you safely inside. I was never one for doing things by halves.'

'As you wish,' said Holmes quietly. 'Just one thing before you do. You acted in a high-handed fashion when you tore off that false beard. Your action was quite inexcusable. If Mr Rhodes wishes to conceal his identity, that is his affair. It is no concern of yours.

I notice that you have paid scant regard to my warning that he is not a well man. However, I bear you no malice, and I take it upon myself to say that Mr Rhodes is of the same mind. What I should like you to understand is this. What I told you I told you in the strictest confidence, and it behoves you to keep quiet about it. If it should get out—and if the Club Secretary forms the opinion that Mr Charles Stewart Caine is responsible for it getting out—then it might very well be that you would find yourself *persona non grata* at the Oval cricket ground. If that were to happen, it would not make you popular with your employers at the cricket almanack. They might decide to relieve you of the need to do all that wearisome travelling from one unspeakable press box to another. Have I made myself clear?'

Caine looked a good deal subdued, and even shaken. 'You have,' was all he had to say in response to Holmes' broadside.

The three of us approached the front door. Caine was dragging his feet a little, having had some of the bounce knocked out of him. A turn of the door-knob and the door opened. We had given ample warning of our presence and a stout lady with a grand, yet motherly, aspect came forward in my direction, and for a few seconds, I felt her outstretched hands rest lightly on my shoulders. She was a head taller than me. 'Oh, Mr Rhodes, you are safe and well. Where did you get to? What possessed you to go out of the house this morning when it was still dark? Did Mr Hirst find you?'

In the face of this awkward questioning I again resorted to the subterfuge of hanging my head, as if embarrassed; therefore, I did not properly see what happened next, but I believe Holmes closed the door in Caine's face, spoke a few words to the landlady and hustled me upstairs. On the first landing he must have spotted a maid. 'Which is Mr Rhodes' room?' I heard him enquire of her. And by that means we got into a dimly-lit, curtained room with a bed, chair, table and wash-stand. He strode swiftly over to the curtains, parted them a few inches and peered out.

I gazed about me. This then was the room that Wilfred Rhodes had vacated in the small hours of the morning. Presumably he had risen from his bed to go to the bathroom. Fatigued, after his exertions in the field, he had yawned so profoundly he had dislocated his jaw. I had never heard of such a thing before. It was astonishing to reflect how different my day would have been had that bizarre accident not befallen him. Twenty-four hours before I had been boarding the train at Southampton. So much had happened during that single revolution of the earth.

I went over and stood at Holmes' shoulder. 'There he goes,' he said quietly. I craned forward and caught a glimpse of the four-wheeler disappearing down the tree-lined road.

'I think we've seen the back of that gentleman, my boy. With him out of the way there is nothing to detain us here.'

'I took a dislike to him,' I said. 'He insulted you.'

Holmes turned away from the window with a tired smile. 'Only because I baited him, and led him by the nose. There was no real harm in him. I would imagine him to be an excellent father to his children, if he has any. Well able to keep them amused on wet Sunday afternoons—playing games with them.'

'He made a mistake, trying to play games with you, sir,' I said with a grin.

He regarded me more seriously. 'You played your part splendidly.'

'Why did you accept his offer of a lift?'

'I quickly formed the opinion that he suspected something, and might prove a nuisance. I saw him as a scorpion, and I wanted to draw his sting.'

'But why did we come here?'

'My instinct told me to obey the logic of the situation. I have done that several times in the past and it has always turned out well.'

'Obey the logic of the situation? I don't follow.'

'No time to explain. We must not dwell here too long.' He fetched a valise from under the wash-stand, placed it on the bed and opened it. It was empty. 'This must belong to Rhodes. Pack into it whatever effects of his you can find. Beware of scooping up articles belonging to the establishment, or we may find ourselves in Wandsworth Gaol. I am going down to tie up the loose ends with the landlady.'

'Another cock-and-bull story?' I said, raising an eyebrow.

He gave me a wounded look. 'My dear Fairhurst, I would have you know that I am essentially a man of great truthfulness.'

'Yes, I have heard you tell the truth on occasion—but your lies are more convincing.'

To that he did not deign to reply and I was left alone. He was gone five minutes and I occupied that time in filling the valise with what I could find of Rhodes' effects. When he returned he nodded approvingly at the valise, packed and ready, and said: 'Baker Street!'

On foot or by cab, we had gone hither and thither all day. Baker Street! Those three syllables sounded nostalgically to my ear— just as another three syllables—Ithaca!— must have sounded nostalgically to the ear of the much-travelled Odysseus. After all, what other home had I—even if only temporary—but No 221b, Baker Street?

We descended the stairs, gliding like ghosts, and got into the street—blessedly, without any hindrances. In the Euston Road we quickly found a hansom and so began another cab ride, which was to be a short one. In the cab Holmes dug into his pocket, produced a pipe and peered into the bowl. Satisfied that there was something combustible in it he lit up and puffed out clouds of acrid smoke. He did not seem to notice that the clouds swirled into my face.

After a while he said: 'The prospect of sitting down to one of Mrs Hudson's meat pies is not a dismal one, eh?'

'I am much obliged to you for your hospitality, sir.'

'Nonsense. I am in your debt—not the other way about.'

'Doctor Watson warned her that you might not be back this evening, remember.'

'Oh, she'll take no heed of that. She knows me too well.' He blew a cloud of smoke towards the roof of the cab and flapped his hand at it, vainly seeking to disperse it. I coughed twice. 'By the way,' he added, 'do not get into this pernicious habit.'

'Can something pernicious be enjoyable?' I enquired pointedly.

'Certainly it can—in the short term. Ask Doctor Redthorn. No, no—let us not revive that topic. You know, I shall touch my half-century next year, and I plan to retire. I have my eye on a cottage on the Sussex coast, close by where I was brought up.'

'What would you do with yourself?'

'For one thing, I should pursue my interest in bee-keeping. When I was a boy I used to help an old fellow with his hives. Apart from that I should live the life of a retired gentleman and breathe good Sussex air for the rest of my allotted span. It might add ten years to my life. Sussex air that blows off the English Channel as pure as spring-water—am I mixing my metaphors? Ah, that is the kind of air a man wants to take deep into his lungs. It is like—it is like—' He seemed to be searching for a word.

'Tobacco smoke?' I suggested.

He shot me a glance, took to sucking the end of his pipe thoughtfully, and made no reply. Soon after he laid the pipe aside.

We arrived at No 221b and I was relieved that we had heard the last of jingling harness for that day. As predicted by Holmes, Doctor Watson's note had not deflected Mrs Hudson from the even tenor of her routine, and we found the fire in the sitting-room blazing cheerfully. It was the kind of English August when a fire was a necessary comfort.

Inside half an hour we were served dinner

and felt that no two wearied travellers before us had ever been better treated.

However, when I retired to bed that night I was not so well treated in the matter of an untroubled night's sleep. In a nightmarish dream I was back at the Oval and stood at the striker's end to face the bowling. The bowler was a demon-faced Doctor Redthorn. His arm plunged towards me. A hypodermic needle hurtled towards me, aimed at my heart.

I tried to lift my bat to defend myself but it would not lift from the crease. I turned and ran towards the crowd. I was lifted off my feet. Angry, ugly faces surrounded me. The word 'impostor' was flung at me from all sides. Suddenly I was at the Marble Arch, by Tyburn Tree. I was pushed up the steps to the gallows.

The hangman turned round and I was confronted by the ghastly-grinning Doctor Redthorn. I leapt into the crowd in a bid to escape. I dragged my leaden feet across the grass. In front of me I saw White Beard, walking with arms outstretched, balancing a huge cartwheel upon his head. Suddenly his legs sank into the ground and he disappeared from view. Now I stood in Park Lane. I hailed a hansom and when it pulled up threw myself into it. A whip cracked and we set off. Suddenly the trap lifted off and there was the inescapable demon-face of Doctor Redthorn. I shrieked and shrank into the corner. I lay back, but there was no back to the seat. I somersaulted and fell down, down, down—until I woke sweating and panic-stricken.

At twenty past two the following afternoon we set off for the conference with Lord Hawke and the others. I was surprised, but not sorry, to learn that we were to walk to Jermyn Street. 'The weather is much improved today,' said Holmes. He was right, and the sun came out and shone brilliantly as soon as we set foot outside. He chose to walk in a leisurely fashion, in contrast with his usual brisk pace, and this was more to my liking, being much shorter in the leg than he was. So we made progress by strolling, which was very fine, but it seemed certain that we must arrive late for our appointment. I suspected that punctuality was not a virtue Sherlock Holmes set great store by.

'Will George Hirst be there, do you think?' I asked him.

'I rather think not,' he replied. 'He paid the landladly and took his valise yesterday morning—that is to say, before the final day's play. Rhodes would have done the same but for his mishap. I have sent his valise to the Italian Hospital, by the by. No, I think, upon reflection, his lordship will have decided there was nothing to be gained by keeping him in London overnight. I think he will have caught his train—after being bound to secrecy, of course.'

I was sorry that I might not see George Hirst again, if Holmes were right. I should have to be content with the memory of his shout to me as we crossed, making the winning run. I had not heard the words because of the hubbub. I liked to think it was not something uncomplimentary.

Holmes began to enter upon a reminiscence. 'This street calls to mind the Park Lane Mystery, in which I was involved some eight years ago. A young man of fashion, the Honourable Robert Adair, was shot and killed through an open window while sitting at a table in his room at No 427. He sat there keeping account of his gambling winnings and losses. He had no enemies that anyone knew of. There were no footprints in the flower-beds below the window. The police were baffled, and the mystery was made much of in the newspapers.

'I had just returned to London after a long period of travelling abroad. In point of fact, everybody believed me to be dead.'

'The Reichenbach Falls,' I put in.

'Ah, so you have read Doctor Watson's account of that episode, which he calls "The Final Problem". It transpired that he was premature in calling it that. Well, in those days I took great delight in assuming dis-

guises. One evening I stood outside No 427
—we are fast approaching that address now—
along with many others, curious—perhaps
morbidly curious—to view the scene of the
crime. I was disguised as an elderly, deform-
ed man. Of all people, who should I spot but
my old friend, Doctor Watson. I contrived
that he should walk into me and knock to
the ground a few scholarly books I was carrying under my arm. He was apologetic and
gathered them up for me, but I mouthed
curses at him, turned on my heel and went
off.

'Later that evening, still play-acting, I
knocked on his door, gained entrance to his
room and, when his back was turned, whisk-
ed off my disguise and straightened my back.
He turned round and fainted clean away—
the only time in his life that had happened
to him, he told me afterwards.'

'Wasn't it rather brutal of you to give him
a shock like that?' I said.

'Brutal? Oh yes, and, therefore, suiting the
low opinion you have of my character. To

my habitual untruthfulness you may now add my brutality. Ah, this is the house here.'

We stood before a very smart address indeed. He pointed out the window that had figured in the case. The house was no longer the object of anyone's curiosity, morbid or otherwise, and ours waned quickly. The exterior, though elegant, now presented a perfectly docile appearance. We continued our leisurely walk to Jermyn Street.

At No 107 we were ushered into a sparsely-furnished drawing-room where we found Lord Hawke standing seignorially with his back to the hearth and Messrs Alcock and Maclaren seated. Holmes was clearly right about George Hirst not having been detained overnight.

His lordship's opening speech was that he had hoped that we would be punctual, and made it clear that he was peeved that his hope had not been fulfilled. 'I shan't offer you a drink, Mr Holmes, as time is short. I have to leave in ten minutes to attend a meeting. I am always punctual when I attend meetings. Ahem! I will therefore be brief in saying what I have to say. First, this morning Mr Alcock received a letter from Doctor Redthorn in which he declares his firm intention to quit his practice and go abroad. If he—'

'I suggest Devil's Island,' broke in Maclaren.

Lord Hawke drew in his breath. 'Maclaren, I must ask you not to interrupt. There is no time for all that. I was saying that—if he were to do as he promises it would solve a lot of difficulties, but we must wait to hear what Rhodes has to say about it, he being the injured party in this business. I visited him at the Italian Hospital yesterday evening and was relieved to find him very much himself. Tomorrow morning he will be discharged into my care and, together, we will catch the noon train to the North. George Hirst left London last night. I had a long talk with him before he went. His lips are sealed.

'Now we come to another matter. At the hospital I met a certain Doctor Watson, who was also visiting the patient. He will not, I think, be unknown to you, Mr Holmes.'

Holmes had started at the name of his old friend. Thus was a surprise provided for the provider of surprises.

'In the course of our conversation he informed me that you were taken ill in the early afternoon of yesterday, but that, in defiance of his advice, given in the strongest terms, you rose from your sickbed several hours later and made your way to the Oval Cricket Ground. I must say I was struck by the pallor of your face, but I was not to know that this was not its habitual state. Mr Holmes, I offer my congratulations on the skill and assiduity with which you conducted the investigation of the Rhodes mystery. These are the congratulations which, yesterday, I said I would reserve. Whether I can unreservedly forgive you for having kept back from me certain information— you know to what I am referring—depends

255

whether time will show that we have successfully concealed the truth of what happened at the fall of the ninth wicket in the Fifth Test.

'Thus far we seem to be successful. The newspapers this morning are, quite properly, ecstatic in their praise of Jessop's innings, and the performance of the team as a whole. The *Times* devotes its leader to the match. However, in my opinion, insufficient praise is given to the showing of the No 11 batsman, whom the newspapers suppose to have been Wilfred Rhodes. I shall not be so niggardly in my praise.'

He turned and directed his unblinking gaze at me. 'I see this young man, who bears such an astonishing facial resemblance to Rhodes, as a prime example of the English club cricketer—the week-ender—playing on the village green from May to September, keeping alive the undying tradition of Hambledon. I salute him for upholding the English tradition of displaying courage in the face of adversity.' As he ended this tribute the other three men present cried 'Hear Hear!' and 'Bravo!' So what could I do but hang my head?

Lord Hawke, after consulting his watch, rang for his manservant, signalling the end of the conference. His manservant appeared almost immediately with his coat, hat, travelling-bag and silver-topped cane. He took them and moved swiftly towards the door, saying, over his shoulder: 'Good afternoon, gentlemen!'

It was then I decided the moment had come. There had been a welling up inside me, and a welling up, eventually, will lead to a brimming over. I decided to take my own, individual farewell of his lordship. Nothing mattered any more. He was halfway through the doorway and stood on the very threshold of departure when I approached him with a shy, bucolic grin and called out: 'Yer lordship—'

He turned and frowned.

'Yer lordship—' I repeated, and now I stood facing him squarely. 'It's a bloody shime oy won't be ible to wroite and tell the fowks back in Austrilia abeout heow I plide for England in the Test Match. Oy'd ha' bin a reel hero. But don't you worry abeout me keep'n moy meouth shut abeout everyth'n. Oy my be a raggy-arse Colonial, but oy know heow to ply the gime jes' loike you English blokes. Well, g'boy, yer lordship, and *good on yer*!'

Grinning like a demented Cheshire cat I thrust out my hand for him to shake, but it went unshaken. He stood stunned, staring at me, unbelieving. At long last, he switched his gaze to Holmes, standing a pace or two behind me, and uttered just one word in a strained voice: *'Tewkesbury!'*

Holmes said nothing. The noble lord turned and went. I tried to avoid Holmes' eye.

On Thursday, the following day, I presented my letter of introduction to the man at the Board of Agriculture, and he informed me that the setting up of the forestry school was under way but was proceeding rather slowly.

It was unlikely, he said, that it would be ready to open until the late spring of 1903.

He said that, in Britain, the twentieth century forester faced the highly important task of restoring timber resources as rapidly as possible. In 1900 it had been estimated that nine-tenths of the timber was imported and it was now recognised that this dependence upon foreign supply was dangerous in a world of increasing political tensions.

We had a long conversation, at the end of which he said he was impressed by me. He would send me, with a letter of recommendation, to have a talk with the Principal of the Royal College of Agriculture at Cirencester, in the county of Gloucestershire.

'You don't want to be a mere woodcutter all your life, do you?' he asked me, with a smile.

When I shook him by the hand and left his office I was somewhat dazed.

On the next day, Friday, Mr Holmes kindly accompanied me to Paddington Station, from which I was to travel to Cirencester. In the great, cathedral-like terminus, and under the glazed iron-arched arcades of its lofty roof, its many platforms teemed with travellers. Just before my train steamed away Holmes said: 'I have lost a most able and resourceful assistant. My loss is the College of Agriculture's gain.'

'It's not certain I'll get a place at the college,' I pointed out to him.

'I was born and brought up in the country, my dear Fairhurst. Countrymen are not fools. The Principal will be an agriculturalist, and what is that but a countryman who has studied his subject more deeply than the next man? I would bet heavily on a countryman to make a wise decision. You will be accepted—you will do well—and I foresee a great future for you in your field.'

I thanked him for his generous sentiments. We said our goodbyes and the train began to move.

He was left on the platform—tall, still and solitary.

POSTSCRIPT

The following is an extract from one of the letters that later passed between the widowed lady, living in Gloucestershire, and the Secretary of the Holmes/Watson Society.

'I knew that he had written articles for technical journals and that sort of thing, but I never knew he had attempted a full-length work of fiction. In his tale he rather leans towards representing himself as a mere wood-cutter, and, of course, a wood-cutter is exactly what he was—prior to his losing three fingers of his left hand in an accident.

' "It's an ill wind…'as the saying goes. It meant that he had to draw upon his intellectual resources in order to carve a career for himself. He devoured every book of natural history, botany, etc that he could lay hands upon. He came to England with the guarantee of a place at the Royal Agricultural College. He studied for and obtained degrees in the botanical sciences; thereafter, he was involved in most of the big reafforestation projects of the first half of the century.

'He met my mother at a May-ball at the college—local beauties were brought in to provide partners for the students, who were, of course, all male. They lived happily ever after.

'The accident to his left hand happened when he was twenty-one, and it must have been a bitter blow to him, as it put a stop to his playing cricket, a game he dearly loved. When his hand had healed he tried to play again, but when the bat had fallen from his hands several times and he had heard an unkind remark from the wicket-keeper (who may not have known of his disability) he vowed never to play again.

'I suppose his writing this tale a year or two after his retirement was a kind of wistful, compensatory flight of fancy. And, of course, he loved the Sherlock Holmes stories and joined your Holmes/Watson Society shortly after settling in England.

'The truth is that he arrived in England in early August, 1902—in plenty of time to see the whole of the Fifth Test, as he had planned. My brothers tell me that he never tired of telling the story of the exciting last day's play, famous to this day for Jessop's match-winning innings. He very sportingly gave full credit to England for their triumph over his native land....'

APPENDIX

In the foregoing story the narrator, John Fairhurst, maintains the fiction that the stories of Sherlock Holmes were written by Doctor Watson ('Well, I suppose he must be regarded as a man of letters now, as well as a man of medicine,' said Holmes—one of a handful of sentences I borrowed and slightly adapted from the original.) Of course, they were in reality written by Dr Conan Doyle, later to emerge from one of King Edward's investitures as Sir Arthur Conan Doyle. This was a popular knighthood, for he was a man universally liked.

It is surprising that there are no references to cricket in the Holmes stories he wrote. Why surprising? Because, despite his Irish name and Scottish upbringing, Conan Doyle, upon settling in England as a young doctor, developed a deep knowledge of the English game and a great and abiding affection for it. When he had established himself as a celebrated author and clubbable man he played a number of times for the M.C.C. He made a century at Lord's and his bowling feats included taking 7 for 51 against Cambridgeshire, achieving the hat-trick against Warwickshire and, the most meritorious feat of all, clean-bowling the legendary W.G Grace himself.

With a team picturesquely called the Stonyhurst Wanderers he went touring in Ireland, the land of his forefathers, and whilst in those lush pastures penned a few light-hearted verses, the last verse of which ran:

So fill up a bumper to one and to all,
Who handled the willow, the gloves & the
    ball,
May cricketers ever their prowess recall,
And may Stonyhurst flourish whatever be-
    fall.

Is there not something of the real amateur cricket spirit in these careless lines?

It is not difficult to find Holmes and Watson, if not inside the ground itself, in the vicinity of the Kennington Oval. At the beginning of *The Sign of Four* we find them seated in a four-wheeler with the delectable Miss Mary Morstan, being driven they know not whither. It is a murky September night but Holmes, who knows London as well as any cabbie, is muttering to himself the names of squares and streets as the cab bowls along. ' "Rochester Row," said he. "Now Vincent Square. Now we come out on the Vauxhall Bridge Road. We are making for the Surrey side, apparently. Yes, I thought so. Now we are on the bridge. You can catch glimpses of the river." ' Alas, they turn to the right down Wandsworth Road and miss riding past the Oval cricket-ground.

Later, however—in the dawn hours of the morning—Holmes and his love-smitten friend—yes, the doctor has succumbed to the charms of Miss Morstan—are off on a 'six-mile trudge' with a bird-stuffer's mongrel dog. The dog is nosing the trail of a dwarfish Andaman Islander who has unwittingly put his shoe in a puddle of creosote at the scene of the crime. The trail leads them 'through the side-streets to the east of the Oval,' but then doubles back westward to the Nine Elms district beside the river. Holmes and Watson are on the trail of treasure, half of which rightfully belongs to Miss Morstan. Do they find it? You must—if you have not already—read *The Sign of Four*.

Hitherto it has been left to the distinguished crimewriter, Julian Symons, to link Holmes with the game his creator enjoyed watching and playing when he wrote: 'Sherlock Holmes is the W.G Grace of the Detective Story.' That is a pleasant tribute. A less pleasant tribute was paid to the detective by George Bernard Shaw when he wrote: 'Holmes was a drug addict without a single amiable trait.'

That there should be no references to

cricket in Conan Doyle's stories I thought a pity, and I have attempted to supply the omission. At the same time I have tried to scotch the charge made by my illustrious namesake that Holmes had not a single amiable trait.

Melbourne Cricket Club was formed in 1838 and interstate matches began in 1856. By the 1880s it was no longer left to nibbling sheep to keep the playing strip cropped. The groundsman's art of levelling, watering, mowing and rolling was being perfected and, as a consequence, the great Australian strokemakers began to emerge.

It is romantic—the notion of the sons and grandsons of pioneer emigrants to Australia voyaging to the Mother Country to show the milling crowds there how to play the summer game. And show them they did. The 1902 Fifth Test was the 66th Test Match between the two sides and England was only marginally ahead in the number of wins to her credit. By 1909 Australia had drawn level.

Australia had had by far the better of it in the previous series, played in the southern hemisphere from December, 1901 to February, 1902, winning four matches to one. There were, as it happened, no declarations in any of those five games, proving that bowlers on both sides enjoyed as much success as batsmen. It must be allowed that English weather is more unsettled than Australian weather. The late 'innings declared' innovation had been a success at home, providing a way through to a result—and usually a fair result—when wet conditions threatened to ruin the game. White Beard's pouring scorn on declarations must be seen to be bravado triumphing over commonsense.

When the new series began in the early summer of 1902 the English Test selectors were confident that, strengthened by the presence of such as C.B Fry and K.S Ranjitsinhji, who had not gone to Australia in the winter, far better results could be achieved. In the first match at Edgbaston, England should have won after batting first and piling up a big total and then shooting out the Aussies for 36, Rhodes and Hirst taking the wickets. The match was washed out by rain. In the Second Test at Lord's play was only possible on the first day and that match, too, was washed out.

The Third Test was won handsomely by Australia. From England's point of view the outlook was not rosy. A supreme effort had to be made in the Fourth Test at Old Trafford. In the event England were beaten by three runs in a tremendously exciting match. In the years that followed, when the match was being recalled and analysed, the England team selection was much criticized and one of the players, Fred Tate, unfairly made a scapegoat—but Gilbert Jessop (who had been dropped) was probably right when he said that no England team can ever have been picked with less regard for its fielding capabilities than this one. Australia shrewdly capitalized on that weakness—and why should they not, for it is all part of the marvellous variety of cricket tactics?

271

The series was lost—but could the home side salvage something from the wreck by achieving a decisive victory at Kennington Oval? The Oval was the truly London arena. It did not aspire to the cosmopolitan grandeur of Lord's. Players were more in touch with spectators than was possible at Lord's. The great gasholders brooded over the expansive playing area and the face of Big Ben could be seen through the smoky atmosphere a mile and a half away.

The selectors wisely brought Jessop—match-winner *par excellence*—back into the team. The Gloucestershire captain was, however, somewhat taken aback by Lord Hawke's statement that Maclaren, the team captain, had guaranteed that he, Jessop, would bowl for at least half to three-quarters of an hour at a stretch. He was not ideally built for a fast bowler and, although only twenty-eight, he considered that his days of bowling fast for long spells were behind him. He lost no time in making that clear to Lord Hawke who, fortunately, took the view that, after all, it was not an essential condition of his being selected to play.

Ranjitsinhji, the Indian prince, who up to that time had been the very greatest ornament to the game, was dropped and never played for England again.

The first day of the match was Monday, the 11th of August. Saturday, the 9th of August, had been Coronation Day. There had been a seven weeks postponement of the ceremony, owing to the need arising for the new King to have his appendix removed. There had been, by way of a garnish to the proceedings, half a million 'dinners to the poor', all round the country—partly paid for out of the King's purse. John Fairhurst does not mention having seen bunting and flags displayed during his travels round London in hansom cabs. Perhaps a mood of 'back to business' prevailed and all the festive decorations had been swiftly taken down once the great occasion for rejoicing had gone by.

At the Oval a crowd of about twelve thousand assembled at the start of play. Who were they, one wonders. Young men of the gilded youth sort? Professional men able to take a day or two off to see the South London Test Match? Shop and factory workers halfway through their annual week's holiday —those who had not gone to Brighton or Eastbourne because the weather was more autumnal than summery?

Australia won the toss and batted all day to make 324—a formidable total in a three day match. On the second day conditions were poor, the wicket having had a good soaking from rain in the early morning—on top of which the light was bad. Everything pointed to a Test that would end either in a dull draw or an ignominious defeat for the home side. However, the dreaded follow-on was saved, thanks largely to a spirited 43 contributed by George Hirst.

At a quarter to four Australia began their second innings and England's luck changed. The slippery turf acted in their favour when Trumper was run out—he failed to get back when his partner refused a quick run. Jessop's lightning return to the 'keeper found the star batsman sitting sadly on the ground. The value to a side of a brilliant fielder of the Derek Randall kind was never better demonstrated. A quick hundred by Trumper—or even a quick fifty—would have decided England's fate. It was characteristic of Jessop, a man modest almost to a fault, that in his book he simply says: 'Trumper was run out attempting a risky run.'

England were now on their mettle, pulling off great feats of stopping and catching in the field. When stumps were drawn Australia had been restricted to 114 runs for the loss of 8 wickets. They were, however, 255 runs in the lead. Who would have bet on England to win the match?

There was rain in the night. When the third and last day's play began, Surrey's Lockwood bowled flat out and saw to it that Australia added only 7 more runs to their total. Now it was 263 to win and an unhelpful pitch to bat on. Pacy bowling from the left-arm Saunders destroyed Maclaren, Tyldesley and Palairet, with only 10 runs on the board. F.S Jackson was joined by Hayward, the local Kennington hero, and they struggled to 28, when the rains came and there was a thirty-five minute stoppage. When play restarted Hayward, to the vast disappointment of the crowd, failed to deal with a quick one from Saunders and was caught at the wicket. 31 for 4.

Braund joined Jackson, who was beginning to look more solid, but after the pair had added 17 in gritty style he, too, was caught at the wicket, this time off the bowling of the tall off-spinner, Hugh Trumble. England's performance had now reached rock-bottom—48 for 5. What hope was there?

Hope arrived at the crease in the shape of the greatest hitter in English cricket history, Gilbert Jessop—the man who, when he had finished his career, left this imperishable record in the record-book: *on fifteen occasions he had hit a century in under an hour.* C.B Fry, in his book, recalled an innings of 53 Jessop compiled in 1895: '...his usual electric impudence. He walked in to bat with a big cap on his small head, peak well over his nimble eyes, at a fast pace and with no fears. He set himself into his crouching pose at the wicket. It was an amazing exhibition. He fled out to drive like an amateur thunderbolt projected by Jove after too much nectar. He flung his bat at the ball like a ballistic flail....'

The Gloucestershire man was seven years older now and did not leap out at every ball bowled to him—he felt disposed to block a few. Nevertheless, there was precious little 'playing in' with his style of batting. He got after Saunders and Trumble straightaway—48 for 5 improved to 157 for 5 in just over an hour and then Jackson was caught and bowled by Trumble. He had played a backbone innings of the greatest value to his side.

George Hirst came in—a Yorkshire professional taking the place of a Yorkshire amateur—and he knew that while Jessop's blacksmith's blows were striking sparks off the anvil at the other end the feature of his play had to be restraint. Jessop was quickening the pace—anything the slightest bit loose was smashed to the ropes. Several hits went into the crowd or onto the pavilion roof, but such hits did not count as six until a few years later in the evolution of the game. He reached his century in seventy-five minutes.

In the fifty minutes it had taken him to raise his score from the lunchtime 29 to 100 the crowd had swelled to twenty-two thousand. This must have been a mighty pouring into the ground and the atmosphere must have been more like that of an F.A Cup Final than that of a Test Match. The great demonstration when his century was reached may have unsettled the hero of the hour. He pulled Armstrong to leg for another savage four. Attempting to do the same with the very next ball he did not quite get hold of it and put up a catch to Noble at square leg. Was ever a catch more gratefully accepted?

Now the burden of responsibility rested

on the sturdy shoulders of the genial George Hirst. Cricket of lightning flashes now gave way to dour defence, with tentative cuts and pushes taking the score along slowly but surely. In this way Hirst and Lockwood added 27 runs before Lockwood was out lbw. Lilley the wicketkeeper, survived two escapes before lofting a ball to deep mid-off. He had done well though, for he and Hirst had added 34 runs, Lilley's share being 16.

In walked the last man, the slightly-built, 24-year-old Wilfred Rhodes. Two York-shiremen at the crease and 15 runs needed for victory. Clouds loured above. Although legend insists that the words spoken when they met briefly in the middle were: 'We'll get 'em in singles,' neither player, in later years, was quite sure what was said. From the moment Rhodes took up his stance to face the sole remaining ball of Monty Noble's over, John Fairhurst's narrative pretty faithfully mirrors what happened, ball by ball, in the ensuing thirty-five minutes.

And so the 15 runs were gathered, not

without a few alarms, and England beat Australia by one wicket. The series was won by Australia by two wins to one. Rhodes said later: 'If George Hirst hadn't saved the follow-on neither Jessop nor anybody could have saved the match,'—a piece of Yorkshire bluntness Jessop would have smilingly appreciated. In fact, out of the twenty-two participants in the game only three could be said to have played and contributed little.

Rhodes and Hirst had started life in the same school in the same village of Kirkheaton, near Huddersfield. They were friends but never close friends, Rhodes being too reserved for Hirst and Hirst too lively and waggish for Rhodes. Both played first-class cricket for thirty-two seasons and are firmly established among the truly great players in the history of cricket. In 1926, at the age of forty-eight Rhodes was recalled to the English Test Team after a lapse of fourteen years. The fate of the latest England/Australia clash was in the balance. Would the Fifth Test at the Oval decide the issue? In

280

1902 Rhodes had played a dramatic role in the fourth innings of the match. In 1926 he did the same—this time with the ball. He dismissed Nos 2, 4, 6 and 7 of the opposition and conceded only 44 runs for his twenty overs. England won the match and the series. It must have brought back memories to the veteran spinner.

He suffered the misfortune of gradually going blind in his more advanced years, but retained a keen and cheerful interest in the game that was his whole life. He was to be seen at Headingley and sometimes farther afield, listening to the sounds of cricket and would nod approvingly when he heard the sweet sound of a loose delivery firmly struck to the ropes. At the time Hedley Verity was Yorkshire's left-arm spinner somebody asked him: 'Is there any kind of ball Hedley bowls that you didn't bowl?' 'Ay,' he replied. 'The one the batsman cuts for four.'

Martin Bladen, 7th Lord Hawke (descended from the renowned eighteenth century admiral) was, curiously enough, not born in

Yorkshire but in Lincolnshire, a detail he did not relish being reminded of. He captained the club for twenty-seven seasons and led it, administratively, for longer. He brought in the White Rose badge of Yorkshire cricket; more importantly, he brought in winter pay for the professionals and devised the means whereby they might increase their earnings by the merits of the performance in the field. It was his suggestion that cricket should come under a single authority, which it did soon after. He organized tours abroad to Australia, Ceylon, India, New Zealand, South Africa—even to Canada and the United States. He was a fine batsman—one of those whose primary aim when occupying the crease is to hit the ball hard and often. His name will always be highly respected in the pages of cricket history.

Charles W Alcock was a not less remarkable man than Lord Hawke, although not so well known. He should be better known. He was educated at Harrow and was one of those pioneers who formed the Football

Association—he was its Secretary from 1867 to 1896. It was he who conceived the idea of a Football Challenge Cup, and he played for and captained the Wanderers in the very first F.A Cup Final in 1871. As if all this activity were not enough he took on the Secretaryship of Surrey County Cricket Club and served in that office decade after decade. It was he who brought a team representing Australia to the Oval in 1878, the first overseas team visit; moreover, the first official Test Match between England and Australia, played at the Oval, was mainly owing to his organising initiative.

Victor Trumper was a schoolboy prodigy in Sydney who entranced spectators with his vigorous, yet elegant batting style and continued to entrance them, on both sides of the world, until the tragedy of his death from Bright's Disease at the age of thirty-seven. Of him it has been written: 'He was the artist batsman who reduced the flower of English bowling to the level of the village green.' Small wonder that John Fairhurst regretted not having seen his idol hit that century before lunch in the Old Trafford Fourth Test in the memorable year of 1902.

A batsman of a quite different order was Gilbert Jessop. No batsman, of whatever nationality, has approached his record as a fast-scoring hard-hitter. The word *Jessopian* is now, for all time, in dictionaries of the English language and while cricket has players of the calibre of England's Ian Botham, India's Kapil Dev and, supremely the West Indies' Viv Richards the word will not fall into disuse.

STANLEY SHAW

The publishers hope that this book has given you enjoyable reading. Large Print Books are especially designed to be as easy to see and hold as possible. If you wish a complete list of our books, please ask at your local library or write directly to: Magna Print Books, Long Preston, North Yorkshire, BD23 4ND England.